Miracle on Mulholland

LIZZIE SHANE

ISBN: 1729651887
ISBN-13: 978-1729651889

For my ohana.

CHAPTER ONE:
THE PRINCESS IN THE TOWER

The Princess of Pop lived in a castle. That was Elia's first thought as the ornate gate slid to the side to allow him his first glimpse of the Mulholland mansion.

There was definitely something fanciful about the estate, with its high stone walls, elaborate landscaping, and twisting scrollwork on the wrought iron gates. It perched on a hill, high above the smoggy reality of LA, like a tiny fairy tale kingdom in the middle of the city. And at the heart of that kingdom was a castle, a three-story mansion as whimsical as anything Walt Disney had ever dreamed up.

Not exactly what he'd envisioned when his boss told him he'd be working for Alexa Rae—but maybe he shouldn't be surprised. Alexa Rae and her kind were as close to royalty as anyone in LA. Why shouldn't she live in a castle?

Ella Fitzgerald and Louis Armstrong were crooning *Baby, It's Cold Outside* on the radio and Elia flicked it off to focus on the job as he pulled through the gates and up the steep driveway shaded by tall trees that helped keep out prying eyes from the paparazzi and the Celebrity Homes Tours that would cruise by five times a day.

At first glance, the security seemed pretty standard—high walls, cameras partially concealed by drought-friendly foliage—but he was here because the diva needed an upgrade so Elia took particular note of the set-up as he parked the Elite Protection SUV alongside a pair of white hybrid Land Rovers and cut the engine, taking a moment to study the estate.

Max hadn't told him why the *Maybe Gonna* singer had suddenly decided to beef up her security right before Christmas, but the timing couldn't have been better as far as Elia was concerned. He needed the distraction at this time of the year—and Alexa Rae definitely qualified as distracting.

His phone quacked with a text alert and he unbuckled his seat belt and lifted his hips to fish it out of his back pocket. The damn thing had been ringing off and on for the entire drive up the hill, but he'd forgotten to sync it to the company car's Bluetooth, and there hadn't been anywhere to pull off to take the calls.

Odds were good it was one of two people—his boss, or his sister. He was sure Max would prefer he not wreck the company car to pick up the phone. And Sefina...well. He already knew what she was going to say.

The screen lit up with three missed call notifications and Sefina's name above the vaguely threatening message, *You can't ignore me forever*.

Elia smiled in spite of himself. His twin didn't lack for determination. She'd always been annoyingly stubborn. He should have known she'd be stubborn about this too. He glanced up at the mansion—which provided the perfect excuse to cut the conversation short when it started to go how he had a feeling it would— and tapped the icon to call his sister.

"Hello?" she answered on the second ring, her voice skeptical, as if she didn't quite believe he was calling her back.

"I wasn't ignoring you. I was driving," he said by way of greeting. "Do you want me to get into another accident and lose the other leg?"

"The amputee jokes have never been funny," Sefina said, unamused. "And I am immune to your emotional blackmail. You've been avoiding my calls."

"Why would I avoid my favorite sister?" he asked, ratcheting up the charm.

"I'm your only sister. Which is why you should be at my house Christmas day. Mom is flying in on the twenty-third—"

Elia's chest constricted, but he kept a smile on his face and in his voice. "Aw, Sef, you know I'd love to—"

"Don't say no. I'm not letting you be alone on Christmas—"

"I have to work," he said with patently fake regret. "Can't be helped. Big new job. Twenty-four-seven through the holidays. All the other guys have families so I volunteered."

"That isn't why you volunteered," Sefina said, the words hard with a truth neither of them needed to spell out. He thought she would leave it there, but he should have known better. His twin's voice softened, but stayed firm. "She wouldn't want this, Elia. Talia wouldn't want—"

"I've gotta go," he cut her off, his throat tightening at that name. "I'm on the job. We'll talk later."

"Elia. You need your family at Christmas."

"Bye, Sef." He cut off the call before she could land another jab, his breathing coming short as he looked up at the mansion.

Talia would have loved this place.

Elia cut off the thought before it could hook into the

7

soft part of his heart that always seemed to ache these days. His niece had been addicted to princess stories and happily-ever-afters, but he couldn't think about her now. He had a job to do inside this fairy tale palace. For the next three weeks, he would guard this castle, day and night, making sure no one harmed the princess inside.

He climbed out of the SUV, studying his new digs. It wasn't the first time Elia had been hired to provide extra security for the rich and famous in the year since he'd been working at Elite Protection full time, but it was the first time he'd been contracted as the live-in security detail.

He crossed the uneven cobblestones to the massive front door and studied the fancy stonework. If there was a doorbell it had been cleverly hidden, so he struck the knocker against the door instead, wondering if there was someone close enough to hear it inside the massive mansion. He wasn't left to wonder long; the door opened before the echoes of the knock faded, revealing a petite twenty-something with pink streaks in her jet black hair, wearing tight jeans, a shredded tee and high heels and clutching a tablet against her chest.

She frowned up at him—the expression halfway between annoyed and confused, but he'd given his name at the gate, so she had to know who he was and why he was there. They'd buzzed him in.

"You're Ellie?"

"Elia," he corrected. "Elia Aiavao." When she continued to glower up at him, he lifted an eyebrow and flashed his trademark grin. "Is there a problem?"

"We'll see." She huffed out a sigh. "I guess you'd better come in." She waved him into the expansive foyer, closing the door behind him before turning with another irritable pout. "Come on then."

Her heels clicked across the marble floors as she marched through the capacious rooms of the castle. They passed through room after room, each more luxurious than the last—and each so perfect that it wasn't until they passed through a room with a towering fireplace that Elia realized what was missing.

There wasn't a single Christmas decoration in the entire house.

No stockings. No tree. Less than two weeks until Christmas and not a sprig of holly in sight. Maybe Alexa Rae was Jewish. Or something else.

Elia used to love Christmas, but all he felt was relief that the Raes apparently didn't celebrate it. These last two years the holiday had been...hard—which was a big part of why he'd jumped at this job, working through the season.

The grumpy woman with the pink tiger stripes led the way to a rear terrace that looked out over a pool, an expanse of fairy tale gardens, and a view of the city below. A small crowd of people stood in clusters around the terrace, but the resident rock star didn't seem to be among them. Elia quickly scanned the group, cataloguing the usual members of a celebrity entourage. Some who actually worked, and the inevitable few who had no marketable skills other than their ability to ingratiate themselves to rich celebrities.

The irritable pink tiger marched over to a table where an older man was seated by himself, eating breakfast. "The bodyguard is here," she told him. "It's a dude."

"What?" the older man looked up, frowning, but as soon as he saw Elia standing behind the pissy pink-haired woman, his expression cleared and he smiled. "You must be the man in question. Big bastard, aren't you?"

Elia grinned. "You were hoping for a small bodyguard?"

"We were expecting a woman," the man said dryly. "Ellie, is it?"

"Elia. Aiavao. It's a common boys' name in Samoa." It wasn't the first time someone had made that mistake, but it had been a while since it had happened. In recent years, people had had more of a tendency to chant his name. These folks obviously weren't MMA fans.

"I'm Victor Mankin. Ms. Rae's manager. Have a seat." He waved Elia to one of the other chairs at the table, which seemed to be the cue for Pink Hair to take herself and her tablet back into the house.

Elia pulled out one of the chairs and sank down onto it. "Is this the point when you explain to me why I'm here?"

"This is exactly that point," Mankin said with an ingratiating smile, offering him a croissant from the basket on the table. Elia shook his head. "Ms. Rae has been a public figure since she was sixteen years old and we've always had security that was perfectly adequate, but three days ago a particularly eager fan managed to scale the property wall and made it as far as the pool before he was stopped. We felt it was time for an upgrade and Elite Protection has the best reputation."

"For good reason," Elia assured him. "Was there a reason you wanted a woman?"

"That was my call," a familiar raspy voice spoke behind him and Elia came to his feet, turning to face her—already knowing who he would see.

Alexa Rae. Princess of Pop. Three-time Grammy nominee and packer of arenas around the world.

"I thought Callie would be more comfortable with

one," she went on, eyeing him frankly as he took in the impact of his first rock star.

Her hair color tended to change with the seasons, but at the moment it was a soft, natural-looking brown, the loose curls yanked back into a tight ponytail that accentuated the sharper angles of her face. Icy blue eyes studied him dispassionately.

Her onstage persona was larger than life, a mix of athletic and sensual, but in person she was smaller than he'd expected, and much thinner, with an air of fragility about her that was tempered by calm, distant reserve. Like she was made of glass, but unafraid of shattering, so high above mere mortals that nothing could reach her.

He was sure there was a stylist in her group of hangers-on who made sure she always left the house looking on-brand, but today that to-die-for body was swathed in an oversized hockey jersey, her slim legs encased in black leggings and a pair of Keds with the laces removed on her feet. She would have looked comfortable, approachable, if not for the ice in her gaze.

Reviewers loved to say that she could light up an entire arena with her smile, but that smile was nowhere in evidence today, everything about her tightly restrained.

She arched a single brow and he realized he'd been staring too long.

He cleared his throat, suddenly feeling oversized next to her. "Ms. Rae."

"Elia," she replied dryly.

"Uh, Callie?" he asked, playing catch up.

"My daughter," she clarified. "Your client."

He blinked, so startled by the news that Alexa Rae had a daughter that it took him a moment to process the second half of her statement. "My *client*."

Victor Mankin stood, smiling as he explained. "Ms. Rae is featured in *Love Me Again*. You've heard of it? The musical? Won the Tony? The film version releases on Christmas Day and Ms. Rae has a number of press engagements to promote the movie over the next few weeks—as well as remind her fans to get their tickets now for the U.S. tour starting in January. With all of that going on, naturally Ms. Rae wanted to ensure her daughter was as safe as possible while she's away."

"Naturally," Elia echoed, silently wondering if Max had known the client was a kid and not told him, or if he hadn't known.

He caught Alexa Rae's frown and immediately flashed a reassuring smile. It was still a job. "Don't worry," he assured her. "Kids love me."

"Isn't that nice for you." Her gaze lingered on his tattoos as she took his measure. He knew what she was seeing. Six and a half feet of brute force and muscle—but while most of his clients were comforted by the sheer size of him, she seemed unimpressed—or mildly annoyed. "Callie's nanny will be here, but you'll be in charge of any security issues that may arise. Not that we expect any. You're only a precaution."

He glanced at Victor. "My understanding was that you wanted a full security upgrade as well as the live-in guard?"

It was Alexa, rather than Victor who answered. "That's right."

He directed his next question to her. "No specific threats I should be aware of?"

"Victor has the threat file for you to review, but we don't anticipate any specific issues." She eyed him again, eyes flicking back to the tattoos. "What's your background? Military?"

"MMA."

A frown floated across her brow like a passing cloud, there then gone. "Is that some kind of special forces?"

"Mixed martial arts," he explained. "I was a fighter. But I've been trained in close protection and security techniques since I retired from the octagon. Only the best from Elite Protection." He flashed her the easy grin that had earned him the nickname the Smiling Samoan, but she didn't smile back. If anything, her gaze grew even colder.

"I'll introduce you to Callie," she said, "and then have someone show you to your room so you can get settled."

"Mia can do that—" Victor began, calling Elia's attention back to the rest of the entourage.

"I'll do it," the ice queen cut him off.

She turned on her heel and began marching back toward the house. Elia followed, fighting a smile— though he didn't fight that hard. There was something about the way the prickly diva's frown darkened every time he smiled at her that made him want to smile even more.

She wasn't at all what he'd expected.

* * * * *

The new bodyguard smiled too much.

Alexa could practically *feel* him smiling behind her as she led the way to Callie's wing. He looked like a badass—all muscle and tattoos—like the kind of bad boy who'd always been her kryptonite, but that smile said that you could trust him, even as it promised mischief.

Which was why she'd amped up her keep-your-hands-off-buddy frostbite performance.

Victor would say she had trust issues. That she didn't like new people.

Victor would be right, but that didn't mean she didn't have very good reasons to have trust issues. People let you down—even the people who seemed nice at first. Fame and fortune screwed everything up. It was inevitable. So it was better not to get your hopes up. She'd learned that long ago. Even family couldn't be trusted.

She would keep the new bodyguard and his too-easy smile far away from her—even if he did make her feel small and—unexpectedly—safe.

That was good, since he was going to be looking after Callie. She liked knowing that her daughter would have that feeling. She might be a total screw-up as a mother, but at least she could make sure Callie always felt safe.

"This is Callie's wing," she explained to distract herself from the guilt that always crept up on her when she thought of her daughter. "Your room will be through there," she waved toward the rooms designated for Callie's staff. "Her nanny, Pilar, will see to her everyday needs. Callie's off school for winter break, so I doubt she'll leave the grounds much, but if she should want to leave you can contact my driver to arrange transportation." She heard herself babbling and made herself shut up. She wasn't this nervous when surrounded by thousands of screaming fans, but taking one step into her daughter's wing turned her into a mess.

"Are you Jewish?"

The question startled her enough that she paused with her hand raised to knock on the door to Callie's suite, frowning at the bodyguard. "What?"

Elia waved around them at the tasteful décor so

carefully selected by her interior designer. "There's no Christmas stuff. No tree, no stockings, no decorations—I was wondering if she was going to want to do Hanukkah stuff."

"We celebrate Christmas," Alexa said, hearing the defensiveness creeping into her voice. There it was again, that feeling that she was the worst mother on the planet. She hadn't *forgotten* Christmas. She'd just been so damned *busy* she hadn't gotten around to it yet. "With a Christmas premiere and the new album coming out and the tour to promote, there hasn't been a lot of time left over for decorating. We'll put up a tree when I get back." She nodded toward the door. "Ready?"

"Lead the way."

She turned back to the door and took a deep breath before knocking. *I hold my breath every time we speak…* A whisper of a song lyric floated through her brain, gone before she could turn it into something.

When Callie didn't respond, she cracked the door an inch, calling, "Callie?"

When there was still no response, she pushed the door open farther, poking her head inside.

Her daughter sat on a beanbag chair in the middle of the sitting room, focused on the tablet in her lap with giant noise-cancelling headphones over her ears. She glanced up, sensing movement at the door, but there was no smile of greeting. No shout of "Mommy!" and a run for a hug. Those things only happened in movies. Instead her daughter's brows pinched with a slight frown as she lifted her headphones away from her ears, as if she couldn't quite figure out what Alexa's purpose in being there was.

Alexa pushed the door open wider and forced a smile onto her face and into her voice. She would not be intimidated by a nine-year-old's disinterest. "I want to introduce you to your new bodyguard."

Calliope cocked her head, staring at Alexa for another beat before her gaze shifted to Elia.

Alexa cleared her throat and pushed more words through vocal cords that suddenly felt tight. "This is Elia. He'll be here with you and Pilar this week while I'm on the junket."

Callie's lashes flickered and she returned her gaze to her tablet. "Okay."

"Okay," Alexa echoed as her daughter dropped the headphones back in place, dismissing her with a definitiveness that was almost impressive in a child Callie's age. "Let me know if you need anything," she said with forced cheer—even though Callie was no longer listening.

Alexa closed the door and turned away without a word, not looking at the bodyguard. She kept her chin high as Elia followed her down the hall, kicking herself every step of the way for the stupid impulse to introduce him to Callie herself.

She should have let one of the assistants do it. It probably would have set them off on a better foot—and saved her the embarrassment of the new bodyguard learning in the first fifteen minutes that her daughter hated her.

"The silent treatment, huh?"

She glanced up at him—her gaze first hitting his massive shoulders before lifting all the way up to his face. "What?"

"Your daughter freezing you out because you're leaving at Christmas." His smile was understanding. "My niece used to do the same thing to my sister when she had to travel."

Alexa wasn't about to explain that Callie's behavior wasn't about punishing her. That the silent treatment, as he'd called it, was simply how they were with one another, the pattern they'd fallen into so long ago she couldn't even remember when it started.

"I assume Victor already had you sign a nondisclosure agreement." The last thing she needed was rumors about her crappy parenting in the press when she was campaigning to sell concert and movie tickets.

If he was surprised by the non sequitur, he didn't show it. He nodded. "Standard part of the Elite Protection contract. We don't talk about our clients."

"Which is doubtless why you're so popular among celebrities."

Though she knew there were other reasons as well. Their reputation definitely preceded them. Elite Protection bodyguards were the best—highly skilled, highly trained...and the best looking. They were a status symbol among the glitterati, where everyone wanted the hottest of everything—including personal protection.

Elia certainly fit that requirement. His physique was more The Rock than Kevin Costner—not exactly a refined look with the tribal tattoos covering one arm— but his face could have been on the cover of a magazine.

For all she knew, it had been. There *was* something vaguely familiar about him.

"You said you were a fighter? Why did you decide to become a bodyguard?"

He shrugged, smiling. "I couldn't fight anymore, needed to do something, and an old friend thought I'd be good at it. Turned out he was right."

Something about the wording caught her attention. "You *couldn't* fight anymore?"

He stopped at the edge of Callie's wing, forcing her to stop too. He reached down and tugged up one black cargo-pant leg—and Alexa couldn't stop the gasp that slipped between her lips at the sight of the metal prosthesis he revealed.

"Motorcycle accident," he said by way of explanation. "Drunk driver clipped me. But don't worry. I'm still a badass." He flashed another smile.

He said it like it was nothing, the same way another man might say *I stubbed my toe*. And maybe to him it was nothing. He clearly didn't let it stop him, this easygoing man with his easygoing smile who looked like he could take on the Hulk with his bare hands. He didn't even seem bothered that his injury had ended his career, simply moving on to the next thing.

There was something incredibly hot about his self-assurance and Alexa felt her throat go dry as she looked up into his smiling face, her own face heating. Was she *blushing*? She couldn't remember the last time a man had made her blush. It might have been as long ago as Dare...

No, no, no. Don't get sucked in.

She cleared her throat, averting her eyes from that smile, and began moving again toward the back terrace where Victor and her entourage waited. "Victor will see that you receive the latest threat assessment and acquaint you with the neighborhood security staff. If you should have any questions or requests, he'll see to them before we leave. Pilar will be your point of contact while we're away."

She was repeating herself, but he unnerved her, this large man with his broad smile.

"Don't worry," he promised. "I'll keep your baby safe."

She nodded jerkily. Callie. This was all about protecting Callie. He and his smile would be gone soon.

CHAPTER TWO:
BEFRIENDING THE LOCALS

The Princess of Pop was wound tighter than a spring—and Elia had the distinct impression she didn't like him very much. Two things he wouldn't have predicted.

He was usually good at putting people at ease—convincing everyone that everything was okay was his superpower—but the more he smiled at her, the more her brow puckered in a frown. Alexa silently escorted him back to the terrace and dumped him off on Victor, avoiding looking straight at him the entire way—and he had a hunch why.

The illustrious Alexa Rae hadn't spoken more than three sentences to him since he'd shown her his leg and the way she'd immediately changed the subject afterwards spoke volumes about her discomfort.

She wasn't the first to be turned off by his prosthesis and she wouldn't be the last, but Elia had learned to let the reactions roll off him. It was her baggage—he didn't need to make it his, though it wasn't always easy to ignore the irritation that wanted to whisper beneath the surface.

"He's all yours," she told Victor when they reached the terrace, turning toward one of the other members of her entourage without sparing Elia another glance. "I want to go over the choreography for the second SNL number one more time. I feel like I keep messing up the third eight-count."

A blonde woman with legs that never quit immediately separated herself from the cluster, approaching Alexa with a bright smile. "It's a weird syncopation. We can change it—"

"No, I can get it," Alexa insisted. "I just want to run it again."

She turned back toward the house and the blonde immediately fell into step beside her, gushing, "Of course you can."

Elia didn't hear what else she said as the two of them disappeared inside and Victor picked up a tablet. "Would you like to start with the threat assessment?" the older man asked.

Elia focused once again on the job at hand, forcibly dismissing the pop star from his thoughts. "Actually, I'd like to start with the system upgrades. Once we have the extra perimeter cameras and motion sensors that you requested in place, I can review those files."

Victor nodded. "I'll email them. Do you need a hand with the equipment? E.J. can help." He waved over a massive man who didn't look particularly pleased to be summoned. "He's handled Ms. Rae's personal security to date. E.J. will travel with us on the junket, while you remain here, but he can help you out in the meantime."

"Perfect." Elia smiled broadly and thrust out his hand to shake, hoping to diffuse any resentment the man might feel over having the experts called in. E.J., a six-foot-four black man with an intimidating frown, didn't return the smile, but he did take Elia's offered hand, only squeezing a little harder than necessary. "I need someone who knows the lay of the land around here."

He'd memorized a map of the grounds and the layout of the house—Candy, EP's tech expert, had given him detailed schematics of where each camera and sensor needed to be placed around the compound—and he'd probably work twice as fast if he wasn't being "helped" by someone unfamiliar with the technology, but his job here wasn't to alienate the security staff she already had. EP's policy was always to work *with* the local talent, not against them—he was only temporary, after all. E.J. would be here long after he was gone.

Luckily, Elia had never needed the ego trip of proving himself to be the toughest guy on the block. He kept his smile easy until E.J.'s grip on his hand relaxed and he gave a little nod. "I can show you around," the other man acknowledged, his voice a light, surprising tenor.

"Great." Elia clapped him on the shoulder, turning toward the driveway. "I have the new sensors in the car. This tech is crazy. You're gonna love it. Makes our jobs so much easier."

Our jobs. *You're* going to love it.

Every word was calculated to remind E.J. that Elia wasn't here to replace him, and he kept up the casual patter as they unloaded the SUV and began the process of fully securing the estate. E.J. began to slowly relax as they worked side-by-side, and by the time they were testing the fifth camera's signal strength he was opening up about life at the Rae Compound.

See, Alexa, Elia silently thought in the general direction of the mansion, *people like me. They open up to me.*

Apparently, Alexa had been relying on the high walls to keep out intruders. The neighborhood had a security guard—but that was mostly to scare off paparazzi—and the house technically had a security system—but E.J. revealed that it was rarely armed, even at night.

"I keep saying we need to use it more," E.J. grumbled, "but when she's in LA, Alexa works from here and with so many people coming and going at all hours, we gave out the code so much I don't know how much good it would do anyway. And half of them forget to arm it again when they leave."

"With the new system everyone with access will have their own individualized code so you can see who's coming and going."

"It's about time," E.J. grunted, as they moved on to place the sixth perimeter camera. He glared at the wall. "This is where that guy got in. Scaled it like a freaking monkey. Can't believe that shit happened on my watch."

"You didn't have the tools you needed." Elia held up the small black bubble that was the camera. "That's why I'm here. To give you what you need to make sure everyone is safe."

E.J. grunted, still glowering at the offending wall.

It was obvious he cared about his job—and about Alexa and Callie. During the course of their conversation, Elia had discovered E.J.—whose full name was Elton Jamison—had been with Alexa almost since the beginning, hired by Victor before Callie was born. He'd already been in his forties at the time, a former police officer with over a decade on the force under his belt. He alluded to his own history, but steered the conversation away from the pop princess or her daughter, his loyalty to them clear.

Alexa Rae would be in good hands—once they got her security system up to par.

Elia's thoughts circled back repeatedly to the singer as they worked. He knew very little about her—beyond the too-catchy tune to a few of her biggest hits. He certainly hadn't known she had a daughter. She didn't seem old enough to have a kid Callie's age.

Eight or nine, if he had to guess. About the same age Talia would have been by now—

He snapped that thought off, refocusing on the sensor he was placing.

He wouldn't have been so eager to volunteer for the job if he'd known there was going to be a kid on site. He didn't want to be around someone else's kid, reminding him of Talia every day, any more than he wanted to be around his family. He didn't want to remember what Christmas used to be like.

Not that he had to be around Callie Rae. His job was to protect her, not babysit her. He could keep his distance and still do the job. His job was the house. The security system. Keeping anyone from getting too close to her. None of that required him to be with her.

But she kept popping up in his thoughts, almost as regularly as her mother did.

Elia and E.J. finished the perimeter set-up and began to work their way closer to the house, completing the exterior coverage. They were hiding cameras near the east wing when he started hearing a high-energy dance beat filtering through the windows on the lower level.

Elia did a good job of ignoring the music—until movement in the window caught the corner of his eye and he realized the music was coming from some kind of dance studio where Alexa and the leggy blonde were going through the same series of movements over and over again.

She'd replaced the Keds with stiletto heels and stripped off the hockey jersey, leaving her clad only in the skin tight leggings and a black sports bra. She arched her back in a provocative move and his gaze dropped helplessly to the world class ass showcased in those tight leggings. God and her personal trainer had both done some damn fine work there and he really ought to appreciate it while he could. It was only courteous.

As she danced, she looked every inch the pop star. Gone was the ice queen. In her place was heat and sensuality, alternating with a flirty playfulness, the coy, girlish dance moves making her seem younger than he knew she must be. She must have been a baby when she had Callie.

"Right here?"

Elia jerked, yanking his attention away from the window before E.J. noticed where it had drifted. He quickly checked where E.J. was standing against Candy's schematics and nodded. "Yeah, right there. Perfect."

He needed to be focused on the job. Not on Alexa Rae and her perfectly formed ass—no matter how world-class it was.

* * * * *

Alexa sank down onto the bench, grabbed a towel and pressed it against her forehead, hiding her face as much as wiping the sweat off. Lisa called out a cheerful goodbye as she left the practice studio and Alexa lifted one hand to wave without looking up.

Lisa was always cheerful, and never seemed to run out of energy or patience, which had made her the perfect choice for dance captain among Alexa's back-up dancers. However it also made Alexa feel like even more of a brat for wanting to snap at her when she couldn't seem to get the damn third eight-count. Like taking out her frustrations on a golden retriever. It wasn't the golden retriever's fault that she couldn't seem to make her body cooperate.

Lisa kept saying they could change it. Simplify it. But Alexa refused to give her fans anything but the absolute best. They expected that from her. Perfect pitch, unflagging stamina, and flawless, athletic, mind-blowing choreo. That was the Alexa Rae brand, damn it.

"Do you need a minute?"

Victor's voice came from the doorway and Alexa sighed softly into the terrycloth before letting it drop from her face and straightening to face her manager. "Do I have a minute?" she asked him, not bothering to keep the bitterness and exhaustion out of her voice. This was Victor. He knew her better than anyone. And he would have seen right through it if she tried to put on a happy face.

He stepped farther into the practice studio, letting the door close softly behind him, his eyes softening with concern. "I can tell the studio you're sick. Vocal strain or something. Limit the talk show appearances to either a performance *or* an interview."

She noticed he didn't suggest anything about cutting out appearances. Even Victor could only do so much.

"No. It's fine." She sighed and stood up, tossing aside the towel. "I'm just tired. Who knew planning a comeback was so exhausting?"

If it even counted as a comeback if you never stopped working.

Her first album had been like being strapped to a rocket—you were in the stratosphere before you knew what hit you. Her second hadn't had the same kind of eye-popping success, but it had been a critical favorite and many of the singles had been sleeper hits, becoming some of her most downloaded songs. But the third album…

They said failure was character building. After that third album, she should have plenty of character. Which was why, for her fourth, they'd pulled out all the stops to put her back on top.

The best producers. Hours in the studio. Collaborating with the most sought-after songwriters. Filming the movie to come out just after the album so she would get that extra promo boost. All of it designed, carefully crafted to prove to the naysayers that she wasn't just a teen sensation who had outlived her fifteen minutes of fame. She was the real deal. She hadn't lost a step. She could *do* this.

"You're going to be amazing. Don't put so much pressure on yourself."

She laughed, the sound that jolted out of her only a distant cousin to actual amusement. "Easier said than done."

She didn't know when she had become a perfectionist. She hadn't always been obsessed with every last detail of her career. She'd used to be able to relax. Have fun. Enjoy the moment. Hadn't she? She thought she had. She thought it had been fun once. But it was hard to live in the moment when it felt like any slip up would be captured on a camera phone and harped about non-stop on the entertainment websites for the rest of her life.

She glanced at Victor, smiling to ease his mind when she saw the worry on his face. "I really am fine. What did you need? Is this about tomorrow's schedule? Did Kimmel's people agree to the acoustic version of *Love Me Again*? I know it's not technically one of my songs in the movie, but I did do it for the soundtrack—"

"No, they loved that idea. It's, ah…" He hesitated.

She rolled her eyes. "C'mon, Vic. Spit it out."

"It's your father."

"No." The single word was hard. Instinctual. Alexa tried to walk past him to the door, but Victor stepped into her path.

"He wants to see you. And Callie."

"No." She moved around him, but he caught her arm—the touch was gentle, barely there, but it stopped her in her tracks.

"Alexa..." His voice was soft, almost sad.

She met his eyes, letting him see the hardness in them. "*No.*"

Victor grimaced, his eyes pleading. "You're holding onto all this anger—and I know he deserves it," he added quickly when betrayal flashed through her like a forest fire. "But it's Christmas..."

She looked down at his hand on her arm until Victor slowly let it drop. She didn't meet his eyes, swallowing hard and moving toward the door. "I'll be in the studio."

Christmas or any other time of year, she wasn't letting her father back into her life. Not again.

CHAPTER THREE:
THAWING THE ICE QUEEN

Elia should be exhausted. An install on an estate this size would normally take two to three days, but he didn't like the idea of calling it a night before he had at least the exterior coverage complete and all the new equipment linked to the control room. E.J. had helped, but once they had all the sensors physically in place and it was just a matter of troubleshooting glitches, Elia had sent him home and continued on his own.

It was nearly two in the morning before he had all the bugs out and could flick through the exterior feeds, confirming that all was quiet in the palace on the hill.

He hadn't had a chance to even glance at the threat assessment, but that would hold until tomorrow. As would the interior upgrades. His brain was fried and he knew he needed sleep, but restless energy left him feeling inexplicably buzzed.

He really ought to be tired, but instead of returning to the room where he'd dumped his stuff earlier and trying to wind down, he found himself moving silently through the house, checking that everything was secure one last time. Needing to satisfy that restless itch that things were as they should be.

The layout of the massive house was sort of odd and disjointed, as if it had been added onto multiple times.

The front of the house looked like it had been set up for entertaining—or to be photographed for magazine spreads but not actually lived in, one showroom after the next. The wing where Callie lived was more cozy, whimsical even, but completely cut off from the working rooms—the fitness studio, dance studio, and a massive recording studio—all housed in a more modern wing that looked like it had been tacked on to the side of the original house.

Elia moved through that modern addition, wondering how many of Alexa's staff lived on site. Candy would have all that information in the packet she'd sent along with the background checks, but he hadn't had a chance to look at any of that yet. Callie hadn't even blinked at the idea of a new bodyguard—but then she must be used to lots of people in the house with Alexa Rae as her mother.

Elia opened the door to the recording studio, meaning to poke his head in and check for intruders as he had in all the other rooms—in a house this size someone could squat for a week without being found—but as soon as the door cracked open, piano music and a smoky voice floated out.

Elia froze with the door half open.

He was accustomed to hearing Alexa Rae's voice on up-tempo pop hits, but he still recognized the soft, slow rasp crooning the words of *Have Yourself a Merry Little Christmas*.

He was intruding. He knew he should back out and shut the door before she even knew she'd been overheard, but something held him where he was, half-in-half-out of the recording studio, listening to the aching sadness of the song. And it was sad. Heartbreaking.

He listened to that sound—the sound of grief and love lost—and he found himself wondering who Callie's father was and where he fit into the picture. Elia didn't pay much attention to celebrity gossip. Had Alexa Rae lost a husband recently? Had Callie lost a father? Was that why there was something inexplicably somber and broken in this house?

The song ended on another aching chord and he knew he should leave, but something—maybe it was the need to make her like him, maybe it was just the desire to distract her from the pain in her voice—whatever it was, something made him speak instead.

"You releasing a Christmas album?"

She whirled on the piano bench, one hand braced on top of the piano as her eyes met his. This was no ice queen—and no pop princess. This was another face of Alexa Rae, soft and exposed. Her guard down. Guilt rose up that he had interrupted her private moment and he began to frame an apology in his mind, but then she spoke. Right when he expected her to order him out, her defenses snapping shut, she surprised him instead.

"No album," she said softly. "Just…my mom used to sing that when I was little." A sad smile curved her lips as her gaze dropped. "She had a beautiful voice."

The feeling of intruding intensified and Elia hesitated, but she looked so unbearably sad he took a half step farther into the room instead of retreating. "Are you all right?"

It was a gamble. In his experience some people, especially celebrities, hated being asked that. As if the idea that someone, some bodyguard, had seen past their public mask was a grave insult.

But Alexa didn't seem insulted, though neither did she answer. She gave a little shake of her head, seeming to shake off the melancholy that had saturated the room, and looked up at him again, neither the pop princess nor the ice queen in evidence, just a quiet composure. "Elia Aiavao," she said softly. "Unusual name."

He shrugged. "Not in Samoa."

Her gaze flicked down the tattoo sleeve down his left arm. "Is that where you're from?"

He stepped deeper into the room at the unspoken invitation of her question, letting the door shut soundlessly behind him. "Anaheim actually."

She cracked a smile at that, almost chuckling. "Like No Doubt."

He frowned, shaking his head without comprehension.

"The band. No Doubt. Gwen Stefani? That's where they're from too."

"Ah. Most people think of Disneyland."

She shrugged. "I was never much of a fairy tale girl."

His eyebrows rose of their own accord as he looked pointedly back toward the main house, in all its fairy tale splendor.

Alexa grimaced. "That's for Callie. When we bought this place I asked the realtor to find me the kind of place every little girl dreams of growing up in. Voila." She waved a hand like a magician.

He thought of the somber little girl in the tower with her oversized headphones, wondering what she dreamt of.

Alexa bent down, still sitting on the piano bench, and picked up a guitar propped in a stand beside the piano, idly tuning it and plucking out a few tendrils of melody, various Christmas songs flowing into one another.

"You're pretty good on that thing," he said, gratified when she laughed at the understatement.

"You think?" she asked, her lips still curled up. She wandered through a few more notes and cocked her head at him. "You play?"

"Not a note."

She smiled. "Wanna learn?"

He held up his hands, her delicacy making them seem even more oversized. "I'd probably break it."

Her gaze dropped to his hands, lingering there for so long he wondered what she was thinking, but then she lowered her eyes to watch her own hands moving over the strings. "Some of the biggest guys I know play ukulele," she commented, but she didn't press him to learn again. "Did you always want to be a fighter?"

"Nah," he said as he sat on the edge of one of the tall stools scattered around the studio. He was ten feet away from her, but there was something oddly intimate about the conversation, though he couldn't put his finger on why. "I got big early so when I was fourteen I was recruited to play high school football for a fancy private school. Our coach had a sort of different approach—one practice a week was all about tai chi and redirecting the energy of your opponent to your advantage. I kind of liked it, so I took more martial arts. Aikido. Capoeira. The more fluid it was, the more I liked it." Her fingers continued to fill the room with soft music as he spoke. "After college, a bunch of my teammates were going pro, but I'd started doing a little MMA on the side, doing pretty well at it, and it all just sort of happened by itself."

She eyed him, her gaze lingering on his smile. "You don't seem like a fighter."

His grin broadened. "That's what everyone said. It's why the crowds loved me. The Smiling Samoan. Freaked out my opponents too." He winked at her. "Nothing

33

unnerves a man quite so much as grinning at him when he's just given you his best kick to the ribs."

She frowned, her gaze flicking down to the area in question. "Did you get hurt a lot?"

"Oh yeah. Nothing too bad though." Her lashes fluttered she glanced down at his leg, hidden by his jeans. "Not in the ring, anyway."

"I'm sorry," she said softly.

He shrugged. "Don't worry. I'm still an amazing bodyguard."

"I wasn't worried."

The notes from the guitar floated between them and Elia realized he may have misjudged Alexa Rae. She wasn't freaked out by his leg. She was…isolated. A little awkward. Seemingly at ease only when she held a guitar as a buffer between her and the world. And sad. There was something unspeakably sad about her.

Not at all what he would have expected from the singer behind the bubble gum hit *Maybe Gonna*.

"I'll get out of your hair," Elia murmured, straightening off the stool.

"Elia…" Her voice stopped him before he'd gotten two feet. He turned back. Her hands were motionless on the guitar now, her eyes holding his. "Callie's safety is the most important thing in the world to me. That fan who got in here—she was in the pool house when he got all the way to the pool. She was right there. I need her to feel safe. I need her to *be* safe."

"I won't let anything happen to her," Elia murmured and her fingers began to pluck the melody to *Have Yourself a Merry Little Christmas*, this time on the guitar. He nodded to the instrument in her hands. "You should record that. It's beautiful."

She smiled, her lashes veiling her eyes at the

compliment. "Good night, Mr. Aiavao."

"Good night, Ms. Rae."

He slipped out of the recording studio, the notes of the song following him out.

CHAPTER FOUR:
AN INCONVENIENT TRUTH

Alexa refused to have a crush on her daughter's new bodyguard. He'd caught her in a moment of weakness last night, that was all.

She'd been thinking of her father, her mother, a time before everything had changed—memories that seemed at once all too distant and entirely too close for comfort. She wasn't sure she really remembered her mother's voice, though she remembered the words, the way the song had made her feel. She'd been back there, in a moment before she learned how to close herself off from the world, when Elia had appeared.

She didn't know why she'd talked to him.

It was easy. He made things so easy with all those smiles. She'd forgotten, momentarily, not to trust.

She'd been oddly relaxed by the time he left. Calm. On a whim, she'd recorded an acoustic version of *Have Yourself a Merry Little Christmas*, just put down a single take and then she'd gone upstairs to bed without even listening to the track.

Then the strangest thing had happened.

She'd slept well.

Alexa never slept well. Even if she was physically exhausted, her brain refused to quiet and she inevitably tossed and turned fitfully for a handful of hours before giving up and getting up. But last night she'd slept deeply the second her head hit the pillow—so deeply she'd overslept and Victor'd had to send one of his ubiquitous assistants to shake her awake.

Which was why the house was in a frenzy. Alexa was running late—and Alexa Rae was *never* running late. They were due to film the Kimmel appearance before she flew to New York for the first leg of the press tour and somehow the act of loading up the cavalcade of SUVs—some of which would go straight to the private plane to load it while the rest of them put on a show for America's late night audience—required every member of her team to be running in twelve different directions at once.

And through it all Elia moved calmly, somehow never being in the way of the flurry of movement as he made his way around the lower level, checking the window sensors and door alarms.

She glanced at him, trying not to catch his eye, but he caught her looking. His smile widened and he gave a little nod, his eyes crinkling. He really was entirely too approachable when he smiled like that. She jerked a nod back before turning quickly away, flustered.

What was she supposed to say to him this morning? Last night had been…intimate. Easy. She'd had sex with people she didn't talk to about her parents. So why had she mentioned her mother to him? Just because he made her feel safe, accepted somehow, like he didn't judge her—maybe that was it. The feeling that he was giving her the benefit of the doubt, even though he'd seen firsthand what a lousy excuse for a mother she was.

Alexa glanced up to the landing overlooking the foyer—Callie used to watch from there, peering through the banister at the activity below and waving when

Alexa had to leave, but she hadn't done that in years and the landing was empty now.

But at least she was safe, right? At least Elia was here to make sure no one could get to her.

She glanced again toward the bodyguard—and caught him checking out her ass.

Her face flamed and she jerked her head back around before he realized she'd caught him looking—though why the idea of him knowing she knew he'd been looking was suddenly the worst outcome imaginable she wasn't sure.

Victor said something to her and she tried to pay attention, nodding with a fake frown of concentration. She could still feel Elia's gaze on her. Not in a lecherous way. Just sort of…appreciative. A warm weight between her shoulder blades and pressing against the small of her back.

It was an unnervingly unfamiliar feeling.

She was a sexual icon. She'd posed nude—tastefully, of course, with her guitar covering everything scandalous—on magazine covers and had fans write odes to her ass, which she worked hard to keep in ode-worthy shape. But in spite of all that, she wasn't accustomed to being looked at the way this man, this bodyguard, was looking at her. Like she was a woman first and a commodity second.

That was rare in her world.

The people she worked with every day respected her. They treated her like the professional she was. Being sexy was her job—the dance moves, the suggestive lyrics—but no one in her real life expected her to take her work home with her. To the fans she was one thing, to people in her day-to-day life she was something else.

But everyone wanted her to be something. Except

with Elia she didn't feel like he was watching her to find an angle, to see what he could get from her. He seemed more...*interested*. How long had it been since it felt like someone was interested in her?

And the way he watched her, like he couldn't help it, like he couldn't look away... It made her feel feminine.

And nervous.

She could *not* be developing a crush on her daughter's new bodyguard. She had boundaries for a reason. But she still stole a quick glance at him. He caught her looking this time and smiled broadly before turning his attention back to the window sensor he was working on. Making the house safe. Which was his *job*. He was an employee.

"—about ready?"

She snapped out of her daze at Victor's words. "Yes," she blurted, even though she was guessing what he'd asked her. "Absolutely."

Victor nodded and raised his voice above the buzz of activity in the foyer. "It's show time, people!" he called out, and the rush increased in volume as everyone headed for the door.

Alexa glanced up at the landing balcony, but it was still empty.

She shouldn't be surprised. How long had it been since Callie had come to see her off? Years? Miss Julia had been her nanny then. That had been...two years ago? More?

"Alexa?"

"Right." She snapped her gaze down from the balcony, moving toward the door without meeting Victor's eyes, knowing she would only see sympathy there. They all knew. There were no secrets in her life, even the most shameful ones.

She strode toward the door without a backward glance.

* * * * *

Elia stood in the background, leaning against one wall in the massive foyer as Alexa Rae and her battalion of hangers-on prepared to depart. All morning he'd been watching out of one eye while checking on and upgrading the pre-existing security system with half his attention.

The Princess of Pop seemed nervous. She'd flicked a glance at him as her people swarmed around her like flies, gathering up luggage and shuttling it out to the waiting Land Rovers. He'd smiled, trying to set her at ease, trying to remind her that she'd liked him last night, but her frown was back and her brow just puckered with confusion every time he tried to smile it away.

When Victor finally called all the stray cats to order and ushered them outside, Alexa sent one last glance up at the balcony, a flash of something so raw crossing her face Elia was sure she didn't know what it revealed, then she turned and allowed her entourage to usher her out the door without looking left or right.

An ache started up in his chest, right beside his heart, pressing against it, but Elia ignored it. Whatever was broken between Alexa and Callie, it wasn't his job to mend it. He was here to protect them, not to get involved with a pop star and her little girl.

As soon as the front door closed behind Alexa Rae and her entourage, the foyer seemed to echo with the sudden quiet. He heard a rustle of fabric and looked up, just in time to see a small figure dart across the balcony above. So Callie *had* been watching her mother leave.

Elia frowned, but didn't follow the girl. He still

planned to keep his distance—even if it was just him, the girl, and the nanny, alone in the massive house. He'd spoken briefly with the nanny earlier, an older Guatemalan woman with a knowing smile who reminded him of the teachers he'd had as a kid who were always two steps ahead of the troublemakers. He'd told her he planned to stay out of her way as long as the girl remained safely on the grounds and left it at that.

He wasn't here for Callie. Or Alexa. He was here to do one job—and right now that job involved door sensors.

Elia bent to his task, focusing on the intricate work. His phone rang once, but after seeing his sister's name on the screen he ignored it, giving himself the excuse that he was working and couldn't afford to interrupt his concentration. By the time he had brought Candy's schematics to life, it was getting dark, and the estate was as secure as he could make it.

He grabbed a belated dinner for himself out of one of the two fully stocked refrigerators in the kitchen. Victor had explained that Alexa's personal chef had the week off and he'd be on his own for food since Pilar was only responsible for feeding Callie and herself. Luckily Elia was more than capable of making a sandwich for himself and carrying it back to the room he'd been assigned.

He ate absently as he went through the threat assessment Victor had sent him.

There were few surprises in the files. The threat assessment was pretty standard for a high profile celebrity—a few overly enthusiastic fans who felt like they knew her and the occasional letter from an inmate who wanted to. Elia made note of any communications that specifically referenced Callie, but there weren't many. Alexa had done a good job of keeping her daughter out of the public eye. Few people even seemed to know she existed—which was even more impressive when he opened the background packet Candy had provided and read who her father was.

Alasdair Tarkington—"Dare" to his fans—had been one-fifth of the British boy band Forever, which had, ironically, only released one album together before breaking up to launch their solo careers. But that one album had been enough to catapult them to international superstardom—especially among teenage girls—and Dare's solo career had only flung him higher into the stratosphere of fame.

The picture in the file showed a boy with floppy brown hair and soulful eyes emoting for the camera— and something about the image bugged Elia. Maybe it was the arrogant quirk of his lips. Maybe it was the fact that he looked young and reckless—and Elia remembered how this particular celebrity story ended: with Dare Tarkington overdosing in a New York hotel room and his fans clogging the streets outside the hotel for days with their shrines to him.

Elia had completely forgotten—if he'd ever known— that Dare had been involved with a young Alexa Rae at the time of his death. Elia stared at one photo, attached to an article Candy had included in the file. Alexa with her head bowed, trying to make her way through a sea of reporters to get to her car after Dare's funeral, sheltered under Victor's arm as the manager tried to straight-arm a path through the hungry photographers. Already visibly pregnant with Callie. At seventeen.

With that pedigree, the fact that Callie wasn't hounded more than Suri Cruise was a testament to Alexa's parenting.

There was no mention in the file of any other father figures. Alexa didn't have a regular man in her life— apparently the tabloid rumors linking her to various stars over the years had been more fluff than substance. It was strange to think of one of the sexiest women in the world as celibate, but if the files were to be believed, she effectively was.

Elia wondered if she was still mourning Alasdair Tarkington—then he reminded himself it was none of his damn business. She was a client. Or, more accurately, the mother of a client. Callie was the job and Alexa was nothing to him. Just a woman who paid his bills. It didn't matter to him if she was lonely. It couldn't.

As if anyone could be lonely with an entourage that size constantly surrounding her.

Finishing his sandwich, Elia carried his tablet with the rest of the background files into the estate's private gym and began working out as he read. There were background checks on Victor and Pilar and everyone else who had access to Callie and Alexa, and Elia skimmed them quickly—though he knew if there had been any red flags Candy would have already caught them.

In the "additional family" section of the brief, he read that Alexa's mother had died when she was young— which didn't surprise him after last night—but then his attention caught on a note next to her father's name.

Anderson Rae: Not permitted on the property for any reason.

Elia frowned and flicked through the next few pages, but no explanation was given.

Not that he needed to know the reason. He was the muscle. The one tricking out their system. Nothing more.

On that note, he shut off the lights in the gym and headed back to his own room. He flicked on the television there as he removed his leg and showered, telling himself he was barely listening to the television through the open bathroom door—but he'd left it on Kimmel and as soon as Alexa was announced he shut off the water and wrapped himself in a towel, maneuvering back to the bedroom to watch.

The interview was first and then she would perform—and the conversation revealed yet another face of Alexa Rae. This wasn't the ice queen, or the soft, sad woman he'd met last night. This wasn't even the highly sexualized princess of pop. She was friendly. Approachable. Her smile a little wry, like she was sharing a secret with the viewer. And the act was seamless.

Who was the real Alexa Rae?

After the commercial break, her performance was flawless—a song from the movie she was promoting, but it didn't yank at his heart the same way her simple acoustic rendition of *Have Yourself a Merry Little Christmas* had.

When her portion of the show was over, Elia shut off the television, checked the security feeds one last time, and tried to get some sleep, tossing and turning in the comfortable bed. His thoughts kept circling back to Alexa—which was good, in a way. Hadn't he wanted distraction? Hadn't he needed it at this time of year? Something so he stopped thinking of Talia?

A piece of an Alexa Rae song he hadn't remembered he knew snuck into the back of his brain and he smiled to himself—until he remembered how he knew it. Talia had loved that song. Elia swallowed down the knot of feeling that tried to clog his throat. Alexa. He would think about Alexa. About the way she'd blushed when he'd smiled at her this morning and the sound of the guitar speaking for her last night.

His thoughts drifted drowsily and he must have fallen asleep because the next thing he knew a hard knock was rattling his door. He came awake fast, as he always did, with his chest aching from breathing too fast, like it always did.

He never remembered the nightmares, no more than he remembered the accident, waking up instead with his stump aching and a frustrating sense that he hadn't been able to run fast enough—though both feelings faded rapidly.

"Come in!" he called when the knocking didn't let up—and Pilar burst into his room a fraction of a second later, her eyes wide and frantic. He sat up, a quick glance at the cable box showing the time as four-twenty-five in the morning. "What is it? Is Callie okay?"

"It's my daughter," Pilar said, barely swallowed a sob. "*Había un accidente.* I must go."

"Okay. It's okay," he assured her, cool calm flowing through his limbs as he dropped his foot to the floor and reached for his prosthetic sock and his leg, grateful he'd slept in a t-shirt and boxers. "What do you need?"

Pilar watched him, her eyes a little too wide. "The agency, I call them for another nanny, but is too early so I leave message." Her English, which had been flawless yesterday, was choppy with panic. "Callie—"

"I'll take care of Callie until the new nanny comes," Elia assured her, rising to his feet and placing a bracing hand on Pilar's shoulder. "Do you know where you need to go?"

"Miami. My son, he gets me a ticket."

Elia blinked. He'd expected the name of a hospital,

but he nodded calmly. "Okay. Do you need a ride to the airport?"

"I have the Uber."

"Okay. She's going to be okay," Elia murmured, because that was what you said when you didn't know and you needed it to be true.

Pilar nodded, pressing her lips together.

Elia accompanied her to the front drive to wait for her car, carrying the roller bag he found outside his room that she must have packed before she came to wake him. Whenever her lip began to tremble, he distracted her with practicalities—did she have her ID for the plane? Did she have someone picking her up at the airport in Miami? Had she remembered her phone and any medications she needed?

He was so busy distracting Pilar he didn't realize he was still barefoot in his boxers and T-shirt until they stepped out onto the cold stone of the front step.

"You must be freezing," Pilar fussed when he gave an involuntary shiver.

"Me? I'm impervious to cold." He flashed a smile so overstatedly macho that Pilar's lips twitched into a soft curl of their own.

"I left a note for Callie," she murmured, calmer now, her grammar back to its perfect levels and her accent softer. "She will worry. She takes things so seriously."

"I'll look after her," Elia assured her. "And I promise I never take anything too seriously."

"I don't think that's true at all," the small woman said as she tipped her face back to study him—but anything else she might have said was forestalled by the arrival of the car, and the return of her fear for her daughter.

Elia bundled her into the car, promising he had

everything under control here, urging her not to worry. It wasn't until the car had pulled back out through the gate that the impact of it all hit him.

He was now responsible for a nine-year-old girl.

So much for keeping his distance—though maybe the new nanny would arrive before the girl even woke up. He headed back into the house, mentally going over the schedule Victor had briefed him on yesterday. They were in New York now. Doing seven talk shows in three days before her SNL appearance on Saturday. It was seven-forty-five in New York.

He needed to call Victor.

CHAPTER FIVE:
A TEMPORARY SOLUTION

"Alexa! Alexa!"

Alexa darted from the studio exit to her waiting car, waving to the fans pressed up against the barriers trying to catch a glimpse of her. She kept her smile cranked up to maximum volume until the car door closed and the darkly tinted privacy glass shielded her from view—then her smile fell off and she turned to Victor with a glare.

"What the hell was that?" she demanded. "I thought Dare was on the list of Do Not Ask questions."

"He was. I'll make sure it doesn't happen again," Victor assured her as the SUV began the slow stop-and-start progression through New York midtown traffic. He frowned at the ten thousand dollar watch she'd given him when she was nominated for her first Grammy.

She'd been pregnant with Callie at the time, overwhelmed by her abrupt ascent to superstardom, trying to cope with the sudden death of the man who had knocked her up and dropped her flat—it had been a crazy time and Victor had been her rock. Her counselor. Taking care of her when her father had shown his true colors.

"Are we late?" She never knew her own schedule on press tour days—going where they told her when they told her and smiling for whichever camera was pointed her way.

Victor grimaced out the window. "Not yet, but if this traffic stays the way it is we might need to rush through wardrobe at your next appearance or skip sound check."

"Because God forbid I wear the same outfit for two television spots in the same day and destroy the illusion for the home viewers."

She didn't know her exact schedule for this trip, but she knew the drill. Up early for a morning show or two. Then straight to sit downs with the entertainment magazines and radio shows—each of which would find some way to bill the appearance as *exclusive*. Photo shoots. Late afternoon filmings for the late-night talk shows. Then red carpet appearances at whatever galas the studio had lined up. All leading up to the SNL performance and the New York premiere of the film. Lather, rinse, repeat in London, Paris, Hong Kong and LA.

"I got a call from Elia Aiavao while you were on the air."

Alexa's attention snapped toward Victor. "The bodyguard? Is Callie okay?"

"She's fine. Everything's fine. All taken care of. Nothing you need to worry about," Victor soothed, his voice calm and steady. "Pilar had a family emergency and had to fly to Miami, but Callie's safe and the bodyguard agreed to keep an eye on her until the new nanny arrives. We already have a call in to the agency we use when Pilar is on vacation, so it should only be a few hours."

"Pilar's daughter lives in Miami, doesn't she? The pregnant one? Is she okay?"

"Elia didn't know the details, but I'm looking into it.

We'll give Pilar all the support she needs. In the meantime, you need to be focusing on the press tour. Callie is fine. She's in good hands. Really, we're lucky he was there. It's the best of all possible solutions since we know he'll keep her safer than anyone else could."

Alexa frowned. "How much do we know about this bodyguard?" She liked Elia, but that was before he'd been alone with her daughter.

"Everything," Victor assured her. "The background checks were very thorough."

"The same background check that failed to notice he wasn't female?"

"That was a miscommunication. E.J. reviewed the initial background checks and knew he was a man. He simply assumed we knew as well. I've reviewed his file myself since then and I can send it to you. Would you like to see it now?" He reached for his tablet, but Alexa shook her head. The file wasn't the problem.

"Callie doesn't know him. Can we...?" She let the question fall away but Victor read her mind.

"We can't reschedule the junket. You know that."

She had known that.

Skipping out on the press junket simply wasn't an option. It was written into her contract and she could be fined millions for shirking her promotional duties. Not to mention the kind of negative impact it could have on ticket sales for the tour.

The album—her first in nearly three years—wasn't selling well. She needed this press tour to remind the world that she was still a rock star. That she wasn't past her prime. That she could still pack an arena.

Interviews and performances and cheesy Christmas specials. She would do them all if it would keep her on top. Keep her supporting Callie the only way she knew how.

"She's probably still asleep, but we might be able to squeeze in a call after your next appearance," Victor suggested.

Bless Victor. Always anticipating her needs. She nodded. "Thank you. I'd also like to talk to the bodyguard."

Victor nodded. "Done." He glanced at his watch and then out the window as they pulled up at another studio. "Right after this one."

* * * * *

After he hung up with Victor, Elia checked the security feeds and dressed quickly, heading to the kitchen to investigate the breakfast options. It wasn't even six yet and the house was quiet. He figured he had a few hours before the girl woke up—

Until he walked into the kitchen and realized he'd miscalculated.

Callie sat at the breakfast bar with a bowl of cereal in front of her, swinging her feet on the high stool.

Physically, she was her mother in miniature—from the thick, dark hair to the unsmiling intensity. He wanted to keep his distance from Callie, avoid unnecessary contact, but she was all alone and it wasn't her fault she reminded him of another little girl.

"Good morning," he said, offering her a smile she didn't return. "Pilar had a family emergency—"

"She told me." The small, somber girl nodded toward a folded piece of paper beside her cereal bowl. "Family comes first."

He met her eyes, her intense, dark gaze strangely unnerving. "Another nanny is going to fill in until Pilar comes back, but they aren't here yet, so until then it's just us."

Callie studied him silently for a long moment. "You're the bodyguard."

"I am." He moved to stand across the counter from her. She'd stopped eating, watching him now.

"What do I call you?" Her eyes narrowed in a skeptical gesture that reminded him powerfully of her mother.

"I'm Elia, though some people call me the Smiling Samoan."

Her head cocked to the side. "Why do they call you that?"

"Because my mother came from an island in the Pacific called Samoa and I'm always smiling." He grinned now to emphasize the point.

"No, you aren't."

His smile deepened. "I'm not?"

"You're only smiling like my mom. With your teeth. Your eyes don't smile. Your eyes are sad."

Her calmly issued statement blew through him like an unexpected gust of wind, but Elia kept his smile in place. "Are they?" No one else had seemed to notice when his smiles had stopped making it past the surface two years ago, but this eighty-year-old sage in a nine-year-old body hadn't been fooled for a second. "What about your mom's eyes? Are they sad too?"

A little grimace twisted her lips. "No. My mom's eyes are scared." He was tempted to ask what the little girl thought her mother was afraid of, but she was already changing the subject. "You're very tall."

"I am," he agreed, noticing the way she was craning her neck. He moved around the corner of the island, grabbing another stool and repositioning it so they sat perpendicular to one another. "And I should warn you

I'm not going to be very good at crouching down to your level—I'm still getting the hang of crouching." He held his leg out to the side, tugging up his pant leg to reveal the prosthesis.

Callie looked down at it, studying it with unapologetic curiosity. "You have a metal leg."

"I do."

"How did you get it?" So matter of fact. He loved kids, their curiosity before anyone taught them that different was bad.

"I got hit by a car."

Blue eyes the exact shade of her mother's lifted to his. "Did it hurt? Were you scared?"

"I don't remember it," he explained. "When I woke up, I was sore and weak because I'd been sleeping for weeks, but the accident knocked the memory right out of my brain." He made a *poof, gone* gesture with one hand...and he didn't mention the phantom pain. The disorientation. The panic. The nightmares he never remembered.

Callie nodded sagely. "I have things I don't remember too. I don't remember my father."

He didn't point out that her father had died before she was born, simply nodding. She dug into her cereal again, still watching him with those all-seeing eyes.

"I don't need a nanny," she informed him after a few moments of silent contemplation. "I can take care of myself. I know how to make grilled cheese and macaroni *and* I can order pizza. I have an app."

"I'm impressed by your culinary prowess, but you're still going to get a nanny." He shrugged as if to say it wasn't his call and Callie sighed, returning to her breakfast.

Elia snagged the cereal box and stood to search for a

bowl. Callie silently indicated the right cupboard and he returned to the island, pouring himself some flakes—he'd expected something drenched in sugar, but Callie had chosen Raisin Bran. He poured in the milk and the two of them ate in silence.

She was nothing like Talia—who hadn't been able to stay silent for two minutes for anything in the world—but somehow she still reminded him powerfully of his niece.

"Did you and Pilar have plans for the day?" he asked—and Callie shrugged silently. "Do you have homework?"

She gave him a look. "It's Christmas."

"Right."

He wasn't sure what he was supposed to do with her.

He knew what he would have done with a day with Talia during Christmas break—decorating the tree, baking cookies, wrapping presents, keeping her giggling—but the last thing he needed was to be reliving those memories. Not to mention the fact that Alexa had said she and Callie were going to do Christmas when she got back next week and he didn't want to step on her toes.

He didn't know what to suggest, not even knowing how long he had to entertain her since he didn't know when the new nanny would arrive—but before he could make another suggestion, Callie slid off her stool.

"I'm going to get dressed," she announced, carrying her empty bowl over to the sink where she rinsed it and placed it in the dishwasher. She then turned back to him with a queenly nod. "Have a nice morning."

He blinked, watching her walk out of the room, a miniature regent in her own castle, stunned by her dismissal—and her self-sufficiency. He had a feeling if she'd been here alone she would have been just as capable of fighting off intruders on her own as that kid in *Home Alone*. Elia wondered if she'd seen that movie—that was Christmasy—then he decided a child being abandoned during the holidays might not be a theme he wanted to focus on.

Luckily he didn't have to worry about themes. The nanny would be here any minute. This was only temporary.

CHAPTER SIX:
A NOT-SO-TEMPORARY SOLUTION

"What do you mean there aren't any nannies available?"

Alexa frowned across the back of the car at Victor as they rode to their next destination, fighting to keep her composure.

"It's the holidays," Victor explained, perfectly composed himself. "Half their usual staff went home to see their families and the other half have already been engaged by other families who knew they would need extra help with the children out of school."

Alexa cursed under her breath. "So what do we do? Are there other agencies?"

"There are," Victor acknowledged. "But we haven't had a chance to vet them—or arrange the usual non-disclosure agreements." He shook his head, obviously not liking the idea of using an untried company. "I have a standing request in to our usual agency and as soon as a nanny becomes available we're at the top of the list, but in the meantime it might be best to try to persuade the bodyguard to keep an eye on her for a little longer. At least he's a known quantity."

Alexa closed her eyes. She wanted to ask again if they could reschedule the tour, just get off this merry-go-round for a little while and go home, but she already knew what the answer would be. She nodded with her eyes still closed. "Okay."

"Good. I'll call him—"

"No, I'll do it." Alexa opened her eyes in time to see surprise flash across Victor's face. Okay, yes, she had a tendency to delegate things when it came to Callie—always feeling like she was making a mistake when she made the calls herself—but did he have to look so shocked?

She held out her hand for the phone and Victor schooled his expression to blankness, calling up the number and handing her the cell. She pushed the icon to dial the call quickly, before she could chicken out.

A deep voice answered on the second ring. "Victor?"

"Mr. Aiavao. This is Alexa Rae. I'm afraid I need to ask you for a favor."

A long pause greeted her words before he repeated, "A favor."

"It seems the agency isn't able to get a nanny out to us right away due to the holiday season. We were hoping you could continue keeping an eye on Callie until we get back from the tour. Obviously we would pay you double since you'd be doing two jobs for us," Alexa said quickly, words falling out of her mouth to fill the silence when he didn't respond. "And a bonus for the inconvenience. She's very self-sufficient—"

"I've noticed."

Alexa ignored the wry words. "It wouldn't require much and it would mean so much to me. A personal favor. We have a call in to the agency and with any luck they'll have a replacement to you within a day or two—though of course we would still give you the bonus—and it's possible Pilar will be able to return before we do. Victor has reached out to her, but we don't have any updates on her daughter's condition yet. We're all hoping it's nothing serious and if that's the case, Pilar could be back in a day or two." She held her breath, the flow of words stopping abruptly.

What if he said no? She couldn't stop the tour. Could Callie join them? Was her passport even up to date? And who would take care of her then while Callie was on stage? No one who worked for her was just lounging around looking for a kid to take care of.

"I guess I could—just for a day or two—"

"Oh thank God. You're a life saver. I'll have Victor send you any information you might need." That task accomplished, Alexa was finally able to breathe—and worry. "How's she taking Pilar's absence?"

"I can't really tell," Elia admitted. "She doesn't give much away."

Alexa grimaced at the understatement. Callie had seemed fond of Pilar, though not attached. Her daughter didn't seem to do emotional attachment. *Like mother, like daughter*. She ignored the dark voice in her head. "Can I speak with her?"

"Just a minute."

She heard what sounded like him running up a flight of stairs and held her breath as she waited—that old familiar friend guilt waking up to join her.

Was she a horrible mother? Leaving her daughter in the care of someone she barely knew? Even if he had been checked in every way a person could be checked these days. Even if Callie would probably spend the entire time enclosed in her room with her tablet, like she usually did when she was home from school.

Alexa felt like she didn't have a choice. Every time she screwed up with Callie she felt like she didn't have a choice, but that didn't make her hate herself any less for making it.

It wasn't just her daughter's future she was working for. It was the livelihood of all the people she employed. Her life had become a business and she had to keep working, keep singing, keep touring, or the entire house of cards fell down. All those people depending on her...she couldn't just do whatever she wanted. People thought that was the luxury of wealth and fame—but she'd never been less free than since she became an international icon.

"One second."

Through the phone, she heard him knock.

* * * * *

Elia knocked gently on the door to Callie's suite, waiting until the girl called out, "Come in" before pushing it open.

The suite was as tidy as it had been when Alexa first introduced him to her daughter. He could see a pink canopied bed through the open French doors, but Callie sat cross-legged on her beanbag chair again, neat as a pin in dark blue leggings and a blue and white striped top, with her tablet resting on her lap and noise-canceling headphones curled around her neck.

"Your mother's on the phone." He held up the phone and Callie frowned, shaking her head. "She'd like to talk to you," he urged, stepping deeper into the room. "Come on." He knew Callie was mad at her mom for leaving over the holidays, but later she'd regret missing the chance to talk to her mom while she could. He'd seen Talia do exactly the same thing.

Shoving that thought down, and the little surge of sadness it inspired, he put the phone on speaker and announced into it, "Callie's here. You're on speaker."

"Callie?" Alexa's voice came through the phone.

"I'm here," the girl acknowledged grudgingly, glowering at Elia. This might not have been the best strategy to win her trust, but life was too short to hold grudges against those you loved.

"I'm sorry Pilar had to leave. Mr. Aiavao is going to take care of you for a few days, until we can find someone to fill in until Pilar comes back."

"If she comes back," Callie muttered.

"What?" Alexa asked, her voice suddenly louder—as people always seemed to do when they couldn't hear.

"Nothing," Callie said.

"Okay," Alexa said slowly. "Well, if you need anything, you can call me anytime. Okay?"

Callie rolled her eyes at the phone. "Sure."

There was a long, heavy pause, as if Alexa was struggling to find something more to say, but at length she just said, "Can you give the phone back to Mr. Aiavao?"

Callie gave him a look and he took the phone off speaker, raising it to his ear. "Yes?"

"Thank you for doing this," she said. "I'm trusting you."

He got the distinct impression that trusting people wasn't something Alexa Rae did very often. "We'll be fine," he assured her—and he heard voices in the background through the phone.

"I've gotta go. You have Victor's number. Don't hesitate to call."

"I won't," he promised, but the pop star on the other end of the line was already gone, called to her next appointment.

He pocketed the cell phone, becoming aware of Callie watching him with unnerving, unsmiling steadiness. "Looks like it's you and me, kid," he said, smiling easily—and she looked at him, like an insect she was considering dissecting.

"I don't need a nanny," she informed him. "I've been alone before and I was fine."

Elia frowned, disturbed by the picture she painted, remembering Alexa's casual *It wouldn't require much* and Callie's unusual self-sufficiency. How often was she on her own? Did child services not pay attention to the children of celebrities? He told himself not to read too much into it. Lots of celebrities had odd relationships with their offspring.

Instead he shrugged, smiling. "I'm afraid I already got the job. You're stuck with me now."

The tiny sage eyed him. "Do you even know anything about kids?"

"Tons," he bragged without a trace of humility.

Callie frowned, visibly skeptical. "How many do you have?"

"Me? None."

Though Talia would have been about Callie's age if she'd lived.

He hadn't missed the similarities—two little girls with thick dark hair and big, soulful eyes. But that was where the likeness ended. Talia's eyes had been brown where Callie's were the same blue as her mother's. And Talia had been all giggles and fantasies, right to the end, and Callie seemed like a forty-year-old tax auditor stuck in the body of a nine-year-old—which only made him want to coax out her laughter, even though he'd told himself he would keep his distance.

"If you don't have any kids, how come you think you know so much about them?"

He glanced around as if checking to make sure they weren't being overheard. "Can you keep a secret?"

"What kind of secret?" She frowned up at him, her head cocking to one side.

He crossed the room to perch on the edge of the couch beside her beanbag chair. "You can't tell anyone. In fact, I shouldn't even be telling you. Are you sure you can keep a secret?"

Her mouth pursed tight, but greedy interest glittered in her eyes. "Of course I can."

He made a show of looking around, checking again that they weren't being spied on, and leaned forward, lowering his voice. "I'm Santa Claus."

She rolled her eyes, disappointment vivid on her face. "No, you aren't."

"How do you know? You think Santa doesn't have enough magic to appear as a six-and-a-half foot tall one-legged Samoan?"

"Santa doesn't exist," she said with exaggerated patience.

"I hate to break it to you, but just because you don't believe doesn't mean I'm going to croak like Tinkerbell." At her blank expression, he lifted a brow. "Peter Pan? Every time someone says 'I don't believe in fairies' somewhere a fairy falls down dead?" He groaned. "Don't tell me you've never seen Peter Pan. That was my favorite growing up. Most of the women in my life say it explains a lot about my emotional maturity."

"Pilar doesn't like me to watch too much TV."

Pilar. Not her mother. He frowned, but shelved the warnings whispering in the back of his mind. "This isn't just TV. This is your cultural education. It's a rite of passage." He stood up. "Come on. I'll bet we can stream it. You can be Wendy and I'll be Captain Hook and we can sing along though I warn you I have a terrible voice—"

"I don't want to watch that." Callie had started to get up, but now she sank down deeper into her beanbag chair. "I don't want to watch anything."

"It's a classic. You don't have to be Wendy. You can be Captain Hook—or the crocodile. I'll be Tinkerbell—"

"No." Her expression went militant, something dark flashing in her eyes.

"Okay—"

Callie seemed so calm, so emotionally contained, that he was completely unprepared for her to shout, "I don't want to—I won't!" and bolt from the room, her footsteps pounding down the hall.

"Callie!"

Elia was too slow to catch her. He gave chase, but by the time he got to the hallway, even the echo of her footsteps was gone. He didn't know what had set her off, but he'd obviously hit a button.

So much for his plan to win her over with laughter.

CHAPTER SEVEN:
PETER PAN, SANTA CLAUS, & OTHER ROLE MODELS

Elia hadn't intended to start his tenure as nanny with an extended game of hide and seek, but Callie apparently had other ideas.

He shouldn't have pushed her about the movie.

She was obviously upset about Pilar leaving, worried that maybe her nanny wouldn't come back, and here he'd been trying to get her to do something she'd said her nanny didn't want her to do. Of course she'd said no.

He'd just thought it would be fun. He'd thought it would have been something Talia would have liked—and he needed to stop thinking that way. For both of their sakes.

He could look after Callie. He knew he could. And it wouldn't compromise his ability to protect her. But could he do it without being constantly reminded of the last little girl he'd cared for? Without seeing his niece when he looked at her and using Talia's playbook?

While he searched for Callie, he'd called Candy, filling her in on the situation and asking for her help tracking down and vetting a suitable replacement nanny—the sooner the better. He had confidence Candy could find someone if there was anyone to be found.

But until then, Callie was his responsibility.

Now he just had to find her.

It took him far longer than it should have to realize he could use the security feeds in the house to track her down. A quick query of the system showed she hadn't left the house—but in a castle this size, that didn't narrow things down much, so he began reviewing the video.

Forty minutes later, Elia opened a walk-in closet off an abandoned third floor guest room and found Callie curled on the floor with her tablet on her lap.

"Hey," he said when she didn't look up, lowering himself to the floor and bracing a hand on the wall to steady himself. "Whatcha got there?"

Her eyes flicked up then, just for a second. "A book."

"Peter Pan?" he asked.

She gave him a look clearly intended to convey he wasn't nearly as amusing as he thought he was. "The biography of Amelia Earhart."

He'd been prepared for anything from Harry Potter to Roald Dahl, but he had no idea what to make of that—though she was the least childlike kid he'd ever met so maybe he shouldn't have been surprised. "Is it good?"

She shrugged, admitting grudgingly, "It's okay."

He nodded, studying her. "You wanna talk about why you ran away?"

"No." She leaned back deeper into the corner.

"Okay."

She looked up then, unsure how to take his easy acceptance. She studied his eyes for a moment, as if searching for some sign of trickery in them before casting her gaze back down to her tablet and admitting, "I don't like to sing."

"Ah." It made sense. The daughter of a rock star. "Are people always asking you to sing? Because of your mom?"

"I'm not like her," Callie insisted—and Elia had the distinct impression Callie didn't want to be. Was this more than just anger over her mother missing Christmas?

He shoved aside the question. It wasn't his business. Right now, all that mattered was Callie.

"Okay. No singing. But you don't know what you're missing with this movie. Mermaids. Sword fights. Fairies. And their nanny is a dog. Seriously. A dog."

A tiny smile tried to take hold of her mouth.

"What was that?" Elia asked. "Was that a smile?"

She shrugged, not lifting her eyes, though her lips twitched.

"A dog nanny. You know you want to see that. A house like this has to have a movie theatre. We'll watch popcorn and eat movies all afternoon."

She smirked at the way he'd mixed up the words, just as he'd intended. "We can't *eat* movies."

"Really? You mean I've been doing it wrong all these years?"

She giggled softly and he knew he had her.

"Come on. I'll even let you pick which version we watch—though the cartoon version is a classic and by far the best. We may have to watch all of them, just to compare and contrast."

"Cartoons are for kids," she declared—as if she was ninety and not nine.

Elia heaved himself up from the floor. "Then it's a good thing we're both kids."

* * * * *

"Five minutes."

Alexa accepted the phone Victor handed her, accompanied by the admonishment. That was life on a junket. Her time was her own only in five minute increments. She dialed Callie's direct number, waiting as it rang. And rang.

And went to voicemail.

"I'll bring up the security feeds," Victor volunteered before she even lowered the phone, doubtless reading the embarrassment on her face. He tapped through screens on his tablet, glancing out the window toward the red carpet they were approaching. "We're almost there."

Alexa nodded, grateful for Victor and the fact that he never judged her dysfunctional relationship with her daughter. It wasn't the first time Callie had refused a call from her, and when they did talk their conversations were always awkward and stilted, but at least Alexa was able to watch over her daughter regardless of where she was in the world, thanks to the security system, which was now more comprehensive than ever.

She accepted the tablet from Victor, flicking through the feeds until she found Callie in the kitchen swinging her feet at the counter and frowning skeptically at something the bodyguard had just said.

Alexa swallowed around a sudden knot in her throat.

There was no audio to catch the words, but on the screen Callie's lips twitched like she was fighting a smile—and Alexa fought down a sudden pang of envy for the easy rapport the man seemed to have with her daughter after only one day. A rapport Alexa hadn't managed to master in the last nine years.

She'd read his background check again earlier, and then Googled him when her nerves refused to settle.

He'd been sort of famous in his own right, before his accident. She'd found articles about the accident, as well as some about the charity work he did on the side, as well as his illustrious career. The fighter with the heart of gold. Who'd had his career stolen from him by fate.

And she was jealous of him.

"Alexa? We're here," Victor interrupted her thoughts. "You can try calling again after the gala."

She handed the tablet back to Victor, swallowing back the emotion clogging the back of her throat. Focus on work. That was what she was good at. "Any word yet on the tour sales? Are we seeing a bump?" she asked as the driver hopped out and ran around the car to get her door.

"Nothing yet," Victor said. "Though maybe we'll see a surge around the holidays. Parents buying the tickets for their kids for Christmas."

Her stomach tightened at the subtle reminder that she was getting old to be a teen sensation. "I thought the movie was supposed to make me relevant to an older demographic."

"And it still might," Victor assured her. "But maybe it would be wise to avoid reminding people of your age where you can. To help the kids relate to you."

She wasn't even thirty—but there was always someone younger ready to step into the teen angst spotlight. She'd tried to reinvent herself with her third album, to mature, and it had fallen flat. This one was about returning to her pop roots—and trying to prove she wasn't already a has-been. "How am I supposed to do that? Speak in hashtags?"

Victor grimaced. "Maybe don't mention exactly how many years it's been since your last Grammy nomination. And avoid mentioning Callie—motherhood ages you. It isn't relatable to most of your fans."

Nothing about her life was relatable to most of her fans. "And when they ask about her? Because they will. She's Dare's kid."

"Just don't say how old she is," he suggested. "She's small. She could pass for five or six."

"People can look that stuff up, Victor. I'll look like a fool for trying to lie about it."

"People can look it up, but no one ever does. If you say you're twenty-four, they'll believe you. At least until you've sold those tickets. Everyone fibs about their age, honey. It's show-business as usual."

The door opened then, time for her turn on the red carpet, and Alexa slapped on a smile as she jumped out and waved to the crowds. Just another dried up not-quite-thirty-year-old clinging to the fading remnants of her career.

* * * * *

"Broccoli is disgusting."

"And nutritious."

"I bet Peter Pan never ate broccoli."

Elia grinned at Callie where she perched at the breakfast bar, frowning at him as she watched him cook dinner. They'd watched two different versions of Peter Pan, along with *Hook*, before Elia declared they were both going to turn into lumps on the couch if they didn't move. Callie had asked to go swimming—though she insisted volubly that she was *not* pretending to be a mermaid as she flipped through the water.

She'd watched with fascination as he'd removed his prosthetic leg to swim and put it back on afterward, giggling helplessly when he'd begun calling himself Peg-Leg Pete, Pirate of the Palisades. He'd been hearing that giggle quite a bit this afternoon, and every time he did, it felt like a victory. He was pretty sure he'd even heard her humming.

"Peter Pan ate imaginary food," he countered. "We had cereal for breakfast and popcorn for lunch. Dinner is going to be healthy."

Callie glowered at him across the breakfast bar.

"Hey." He pointed a broccoli floret at her. "Don't mess with Santa. He's updating the naughty and nice lists daily."

Callie rolled her eyes. "You aren't Santa."

"Are you sure?"

"Yes."

Elia set down the broccoli, snapping his fingers. "That's it. That's who you remind me of. Natalie Wood."

"Who?"

"*Miracle on 34th Street*. We'll have to watch that one next. It's about a little girl who doesn't believe in Santa Claus. Sound familiar?"

Callie narrowed her eyes. "I didn't say I didn't believe in Santa. I said *you* weren't Santa."

"Huh. That's funny. I seem to remember you saying Santa didn't exist." He began chopping florets.

She blushed, fiddling with the tablet that was never far from her hand. A little girl who wanted so badly to believe but didn't quite trust it.

"Keeping your options open just in case he's real? Good strategy. You should probably eat this broccoli, just to be safe."

She made a face, but when he put the plate in front of her fifteen minutes later, she ate every bite of broccoli, grimacing the entire time. And when he suggested they watch *Miracle on 34th Street*, she didn't even feign disinterest.

He was growing on her, the somber little girl in her castle.

She watched the movie with rapt attention—clearly on Team Natalie the whole way with regards to the *Is he or isn't he Santa* argument—and when Susan got her Christmas wish in the end, she bit her lip, staring at the screen with intense concentration.

Elia waited until the credits had finished and the screen had returned to the streaming service's movie poster before leaning back in his chair and saying, "Tell me the truth. Is Natalie Wood your spirit animal?"

Callie frowned at him. "I don't know what that is."

"You look like her a little," Elia commented, his gaze flicking from the girl on the poster to the girl at his side. "Of course, people are always saying your mom looks like her and you're the spitting image of your mom."

Callie glowered.

"I know you're mad at your mom for being gone, but she'll be back soon."

"She'll just go on tour again. She always goes on tour."

"Do you ever go with her?"

"It isn't the place for a child," Callie said, with the air of quoting something she'd heard a dozen times, her gaze locked on the movie poster with Kris Kringle and Susan. "You don't even look like Santa," she muttered. "At least he looks like him."

"Santa's magic has had to grow more sophisticated over the years. We'll watch *The Santa Clause* tomorrow. You'll see."

Binge-streaming Christmas movies might not be the most responsible form of babysitting, but it was Christmas break and he wasn't exactly a professional nanny so he figured he could make his own rules. As long as they ate at regular intervals and exercised whenever her eyes started to glaze over, he figured he was doing a decent job. Apparently if left to her own devices, Callie had a tendency to read autobiographies of famous women, so he figured rotting her brain wasn't an imminent threat.

"I guess," she mumbled. So guarded. So careful not to let anyone in.

"You should tell me what you want for Christmas. Santa needs to know these things."

"I don't want anything," she mumbled, and his chest ached.

"Are you sure? Nothing in the whole world?"

She shook her head and his heart double-clutched. She lived in a fairy kingdom and had every privilege money could buy, but he wasn't sure he'd ever met anyone who seemed more lonely. Was it just because her mother was gone and so was Pilar? Everything familiar taken away from her for the holidays? Or was something else going on?

Elia studied her, this girl alone in her castle—and her jaw practically unhinged on a giant yawn. He stood up, stretching the stiffness out of his muscles. "Come on. Bedtime."

"It's early," she complained.

"You can read about Amelia Earhart until you fall asleep," he promised, positive she'd be out cold by the middle of the first page.

Callie grumbled, but climbed the stairs from the basement media room up to her wing and trudged into her bedroom to put on her pajamas and brush her teeth. Elia lingered in the overly tidy playroom—which looked more like an English matron's formal sitting room than the domain of a nine-year-old.

"Goodnight, Elia," Callie called and he turned to find her peeking through the bedroom door.

"Goodnight, Callie," he said, remembering another time. Another little girl. Another bedtime ritual—this one filled with elaborate princess stories and twenty-seven pleas for snacks and water and just one more song. They were so different, Talia and Callie, but both of them seemed to know how to reach into his chest and wrap their little hands around his heart.

He wandered the house, checking the security system, but also trying to outdistance the memories that seemed especially persistent tonight.

This was why he hadn't wanted to spend the holidays with his family this year. He didn't want to remember. Last year had been rough. The first Christmas without Talia. He couldn't go through another year where all he could think about was the little girl who should have been there, if there was any justice in the world.

His phone vibrated in his pocket and he pulled it out, grateful for the distraction, and saw Victor's name on the screen—but it wasn't Victor who responded when he answered.

"Mr. Aiavao?" Alexa's rasp thrummed against his eardrums.

"Elia's fine, you know."

"Elia." She cleared her throat, as if speaking his name made her nervous. "I don't want you to think I'm checking up on you. I just wanted to make sure Callie was doing all right. I'm sorry to call so late. I just got out of this gala—"

Something that had been tightening in his chest all day loosened a little. Victor had sent him a copy of her schedule. He knew she was booked every second of every day, but she was still thinking of Callie while she was away. There had to be hope for the two of them. "It isn't that late here. Callie just went to bed. You just missed her."

"Right. Time zones. But she's doing okay?"

"She misses you." Alexa made a little sound he couldn't interpret. "But yeah, she's doing all right. Though I probably showed her more television today than she's seen in the last year. We had a Peter Pan marathon and then watched *Miracle on 34th Street*. I couldn't believe she'd never seen them."

* * * * *

I didn't know she'd never seen them.

Alexa closed her eyes, leaning her forehead against the chilled glass of the penthouse suite, guilt making her feel flushed. What kind of mother didn't know that her daughter had never seen *Peter Pan*?

The kind that spends her entire life on tour.

"Alexa?"

"I'm here."

"I'm sorry. I know she isn't supposed to watch much TV—"

"No, it's fine. It's Christmas. I want her to enjoy herself." *And maybe it will be easier for her to do that if I'm not there with her.* Her throat tightened and she kept her eyes squeezed shut, picturing Callie rather than the Manhattan lights outside her window. She still wore the gown she'd worn to the gala today, but she should take it off before it wrinkles. Her stylist probably had to give it back.

Did Elia know about that stuff? About wearing clothes that were never yours and shoes that didn't quite fit because you were selling an image?

"I Googled you," she heard herself blurting, out of the blue. "Elia Aiavao. You were famous."

"Kind of," he admitted. "Not like you." She frowned, silent for so long he asked, "What?"

"I don't know. It just feels weird. You used to be a famous fighter and now you're watching my kid. Are you sure you're okay with this?"

"It's not entirely out character. I had a niece. Light of my life. Callie reminds me of her a little."

She held her breath, nervous at the intimacy that seemed to flow through the phone—and scared to ask what had happened to his niece. Scared to know and scared of what she would tell him in return. "I…"

"Alexa?"

"I'm here."

"Callie's fine," he assured her. "Do what you need to do and we'll be here when you get home."

"Okay," she whispered.

She didn't know why, but she was suddenly certain he was smiling on the other end of the phone. As if she could hear it. "Okay."

CHAPTER EIGHT:
HELLO, HONG KONG!

Alexa leaned against the window of the limousine, hoping she looked glamorous rather than as exhausted and jetlagged as she was. Twelve more hours. The whirlwind, around-the-world press tour was almost over. Tonight she would walk down the Hong Kong Walk of Fame for the Asian premiere's red carpet, smiling for the cameras and thanking her lucky stars that she didn't have to be eloquent since her translator would be doing most of her talking.

She was too tired for eloquence.

She just wanted to get home and crawl into bed for a week, and see Callie. And Elia.

Her daughter still wasn't taking her calls—which didn't surprise her—but she'd gotten in the habit of checking in with the bodyguard at the end of her day, regardless of what time it was in Los Angeles, and she was oddly excited about seeing him again. They hadn't managed to find another nanny, but Pilar's daughter— who had been sent into early labor by a car accident, though Alexa knew few of the details beyond that—was now apparently out of the hospital, home and healthy with a new baby girl, and the nanny was scheduled to come back right after Christmas. Elia had said he could stay until then. Everything was working out as well as could be expected and she was sort of...excited about spending the holidays with him. At least she thought that was what she felt under seven layers of exhaustion.

As long as she didn't think about the fact that she had to go on tour again less than two weeks into January. At least the ticket sales were starting to pick up. It looked like Victor's gamble had worked. The early reviews for the film were positive, people were saying she could actually act—which was a testament to the director more than to her—and her fans seemed to have remembered that they loved her and started downloading her songs again.

Everything was going exactly as planned. If only she wasn't so *tired*.

The idea of traveling again, of months without end on a tour bus or a plane...

"Do you think I could do Broadway?" she asked, as she stared out the window at another city she hadn't had time to see.

Her manager looked up from his tablet, frowning. "Like, in New York?"

"I'd have a regular schedule." She could see Callie every day. Like a real mom. Not that Callie would want to see her, but maybe if she was around more... "They do celebrity casting all the time, don't they?"

"Eight shows a week for tiny audiences when you could be filling arenas?"

"But then I'd get to go home—no more travel. No more flights at three a.m. to get to the next city for the next show." It sounded like heaven. "I could buy a place in New York."

Victor smiled. "You going for the EGOT now?"

Emmy, Grammy, Oscar, Tony... Alexa snorted. "No one is going to give me an Oscar." Let alone the other awards. She always felt like the two Grammys on display in her studio were some sort of cosmic fluke.

"Don't be so sure. There's a lot of buzz around the song you co-wrote for the credits. I know the Golden Globes ignored it, but the Oscars are a whole different ballgame."

"As if I need to be campaigning for an Oscar in the middle of the tour." One more thing to worry about. She closed her eyes, feeling the movement of the car and almost falling asleep for a microsecond.

"You're just tired." His voice was gentle. Encouraging. "You love touring."

"Do I?"

She had, at one point. It had been all she wanted—to be in that arena with her fans screaming so loud they couldn't hear the music. But now...did she want that anymore? Did she even know what she wanted anymore? When was the last time she'd looked forward to a show? When was the last time she'd looked forward to anything? She was so tired...

"Hey." Victor's hand closed over hers with a reassuring squeeze. "You'll feel better once you get back on the road. I know it's been stressful, trying to stage a comeback, but soon you'll be back on top. Right where you belong and it'll all be worth it."

Will it? The words echoed in her head, unspoken.

"The plan is working," he assured her. "This is exactly what we wanted to happen. Ticket sales and downloads are up. The movie is going to be a hit. You're doing it, Alexa. You're transitioning from teen star to mature triple threat. Just like we always talked about. This is your dream."

He was right. It had been her dream. So when had she stopped dreaming it?

The car moved again, inching forward in the line—and she realized she was next to unload onto the red carpet.

"Alexa?" Victor asked, and she heard the concern in his voice that his golden girl wasn't feeling so golden.

"I'm fine," she assured him, forcing a smile that barely made it to her mouth. "It's just been a long week."

"You'll be home soon."

She nodded, without the energy to do more.

Home. With her daughter and Elia. And maybe this time her daughter wouldn't hate her. Maybe...

* * * * *

"Callie?"

Elia frowned as his voice seemed to echo through the house. The last week had been good. They'd watched movies, played games. Callie had taught him a ridiculous amount about Amelia Earhart and he'd taught her tai chi. She'd started opening up and acting more like a kid, though she continued to be an intense, quiet version of a small human.

Alexa was due back tomorrow and Pilar was returning after Christmas. He'd thought they were on the home stretch, but she'd been reading on her tablet when he'd gone to make them sandwiches for lunch and when he got back to her suite she was nowhere to be seen.

He pulled up the security app on his phone, reconfirming that there was no one else on the grounds and none of the exterior sensors had been tripped so Callie must still be inside somewhere, even if she wasn't answering.

Why wasn't she answering?

He quickly searched the house, but he didn't find her in any of the usual spots.

The media room where they'd marathoned Christmas movies over the last week was empty. The pool where she'd insisted she was *not* pretending to be a mermaid was undisturbed. No small feet dangled from the branches of the tree she'd shown him she knew how to climb.

Elia wasn't *worried*, per se, but his heart was beating a little faster with each empty room as he climbed the stairs to the top floor, with the guest room with the empty closet where she'd hidden that first day. She hadn't hidden from him since. Everything had been going so well. What could have happened while he was making sandwiches?

The door to the closet was slightly ajar and it moved slightly inward when he tapped on it, revealing Callie huddled on the floor with her arms wrapped around her knees and the tablet sitting on the carpet beside her feet.

"Hey." He came in, awkwardly levering himself down to the floor with the help of a hand braced against the wall. "What happened? Are we boycotting sandwiches now?"

A week ago she would have looked away, but now she looked up at him, the words coming slowly—as her trust had. "It's not the sandwiches."

"You want to tell me what it is?" Her mom was coming home tomorrow. He'd thought she would be excited.

She shrugged one shoulder, her gaze dropping down—to the tablet. He followed her gaze, expecting to see the pages of the Earhart book, but instead it was frozen on an image of her mother on what looked like a late night talk show set.

Callie rarely spoke about her mother, avoiding the topic whenever Elia brought it up—so he'd stopped bringing it up with her since that first day. It was obvious they had a complicated relationship and he was no child psychologist. He wasn't qualified to untangle it.

He cleared his throat. "I didn't know you watched that show," he commented, trying to keep it neutral and avoid the minefield he could sense beneath this conversation.

She shrugged. "Sometimes."

"Good interview?"

Her mouth twisted and he suddenly saw tears glimmering in her eyes.

"Hey." He scooted closer, gently gripping her shoulder with one hand, but she was already scrubbing away the moisture with an angry swipe.

Callie tapped the screen and the video came to life, breaking into the middle of the host's question.

"—daughter, too?"

Alexa's smile was all poise. *"It is tough. Being a single mom. Especially when you have to travel as much as I have to for work. But she's the light of my life."*

That sounded pretty good. But Callie wasn't smiling.

"How old is she now?" the host followed up.

"Six. And so smart. She constantly amazes me."

Elia cringed as Callie paused the video in disgust. "No wonder she thinks I'm smart. *For a six year old.*"

Minefield. Huge minefield.

"Maybe she misspoke..." Elia tried, but there was nothing to say and he knew it. Did Alexa really not know how old Callie was? That didn't add up. He'd known there was something off about their relationship, but she'd called every night, checking in. She'd seemed to care. For her to not know... something wasn't computing.

"She doesn't even know how old I am." Callie sniffed, hugging her knees, huddling in tighter on herself. "I hate her."

"Hey, don't say that—"

"I do. She doesn't care about me. She only cares about money and singing. She's like Scrooge." They'd just watched *A Muppet Christmas Carol* last night.

"Scrooge changes," Elia reminded her softly, even as he wondered if he was doing the right thing. He didn't want this little girl to lose hope—but he also didn't know if he should be encouraging her to put her faith in her mother again. He didn't want to set her up for more disappointment, but he had to believe Alexa really cared about her daughter. Though he couldn't help remembering Callie's calm declaration that her mother would just leave again, like she always did, and the girl's soft voice saying Pilar's family came first for her. Who did Callie come first to?

"Maybe there will be a Christmas miracle," he murmured when Callie didn't speak.

"There's no such thing."

"Sure there is. Have you learned nothing from all the Christmas movies we've watched in the last week?" Though admittedly, her favorite by far had nothing to do with magic. She'd wanted to watch *Home Alone* four times—and probably would have watched it again if he hadn't vetoed it. She certainly related to Kevin being left behind in the big house.

"They're *fake*. It's all fake."

"Maybe. But all that belief has to start somewhere. Maybe there's a kernel of truth to all the hype about Christmas magic. Trust Santa."

She rolled her eyes—as she did every time he

claimed to be Santa Claus. "If you're Santa, grant my Christmas wish."

"I thought you didn't have one. What's your wish?" he asked, on a surge of hope that she was daring to wish at all—that felt like important progress.

She met his eyes, challenge bright in her gaze—so like her mother's. "Make it snow."

He lifted one eyebrow. "This is LA."

She smirked. "That's why it would be a miracle."

"You think you've stumped me, but Santa loves a challenge."

She rolled her eyes—which, thankfully, were no longer filled with tears. "Sure he does."

Elia didn't actually know how Santa felt about a challenge, but he had never backed down from one. He'd told himself he wouldn't get involved, that he would keep his distance, but he should have known how impossible that would be the second he met Callie, this lonely little girl in her castle on a hill.

Someone needed to talk to Alexa about what her absences were doing to her daughter. Maybe it wasn't his place. Maybe it was none of his business, but he couldn't just keep quiet.

The people around her had to see that her relationship with her daughter was seriously messed up, but they were all so busy sucking up to the star, parasites on her power, that no one told her that something was wrong. Someone needed to tell her.

Elia had always been laid back—even when he was a professional fighter, he'd had the nickname the Smiling Samoan because the aggression around him always just seemed to roll right off him like water off a duck's back. His greatest skill was convincing everyone that everything was okay. Always with a smile. Always smoothing it over. But sometimes it wasn't okay.

This was different. He'd found something that wouldn't roll off.

The more he thought about it—and the expression on Callie's face as she watched the interview, so heartbreakingly bitter for a nine-year-old—the angrier he became. No one had the right to make that little girl feel anything other than valued and loved, damn it. Especially not her famous mother.

Some things he couldn't change. Like Talia's illness and the stupid senselessness of her loss. But some things he could still do. It was time for him to stop smiling and making everything seem okay and time to start working toward making things actually okay.

Callie deserved that much.

And in the meantime, he'd see about researching snow making machines. The girl needed a little Christmas magic in her life.

CHAPTER NINE:
TIMING IS EVERYTHING

"Do you want me to come in with you?"

Alexa shook her head as they pulled through the gates, catching her first glimpse of her house in what felt like a lifetime. Weather delays had plagued their return and her body had lost all sense of what time it was, but it had to be late and Victor must want to get home and get to sleep as badly as she did. "No. I'm just going to crash. I'll see you tomorrow. Or the next day. Whenever I wake up."

"Don't forget we still have the LA premiere and the press blitz leading up to it."

She groaned, closing her eyes. "How many premieres can one movie have?"

"A lot. But this is the last one. You're almost done. Mindy and her team will be by tomorrow at nine to get you ready—"

"Can we not talk about this right now?" she interrupted, feeling like a diva for cutting him off but just needing five seconds when they weren't talking about her schedule and all the demands on her time. "Can I just sleep and pretend there's nothing waiting for me tomorrow?"

"Absolutely. Get some rest. I'll see you in the morning."

The car pulled to a stop at her front door and Alexa climbed out without waiting for the driver to circle around. She grabbed her go bag, slinging it over her shoulder, and gave Victor a weary wave before trudging up the steps. The rest of her luggage was God knew where, probably following in another SUV, but at the moment she didn't care. That crap was all packed by the stylists. The go bag was hers. The bare essentials she needed from night to night, hotel to hotel. Sleepshirt. Toothbrush. Phone. Just the basics.

The car waited until she tapped her code into the keypad beside the door and pushed it open before driving away. The house was quiet and dark—thank God. She'd missed Callie, but she just couldn't take one more thing today—and her reunions with her daughter were invariably another source of stress.

She kicked the door shut behind her, hearing the locks click, and toed off her shoes, the cool marble floor heaven against her bare feet.

She'd sleep tonight. Some nights the insomnia would keep her awake for hours, but she was so exhausted, she'd be lucky if she made it to her bed before she passed out.

Movement on the balcony called her attention toward Callie's wing and her throat tightened at the thought of facing her daughter, but the shape that emerged through the shadows was too large to be Callie. Moonlight filtered in through the large windows over the front door, lending the space a strange intimacy, as the bodyguard appeared on the balcony above her.

"Elia…" He wore a loose pair of shorts and a white undershirt. The metal of his prosthesis glinted in the moonlight and her gaze caught on the tattoos that worked down one arm as he descended the stairs. She wet her lips. "Is everything all right with Callie?"

"She's fine. She's asleep." Then he stopped, two steps above her, his hand tightening on the railing, and shook his head sharply, as if shaking away a fly. "Actually, that's a lie. She isn't fine."

Her throat tightened with fear and dread. "What happened?"

"Do you know she watches you?" he asked. "Your interviews?"

She shook her head, too tired to try to puzzle out what he meant. "I don't know what you—"

"Did you really think she wouldn't hear the way you talk about her?"

How do I talk about her? She frowned. "Elia. It's late—"

"She saw you," he interrupted, his voice hard. "When you told the American viewing public that she was six."

Alexa closed her eyes, suddenly feeling sick to her stomach. "She wasn't supposed to see that."

"Do you seriously not know how old your own daughter is?"

"Of course I do," she said, the words coming out more tired than sharp. She scrubbed a hand down her face and slipped past him up the stairs. "I had my reasons."

"Oh. Well. I guess if you had your reasons, that's fine then."

She froze on the stairs above him, gripping the railing hard, the muscles in her neck tightening as anger penetrated her exhaustion. "I don't have to explain myself to you."

"No?" He didn't move and she didn't turn back, but she could feel him behind her, *feel* the condemnation in his eyes. "What about Callie? Do you explain yourself to her?"

She should have walked away. He was nothing. No one. So what if she'd liked him, trusted him?

So what if she deserved every word he was saying?

She should have kept walking. But she looked over her shoulder, turning, defensiveness sharpening her words into tiny blades. "What does it matter how old the public thinks she is? I've worked hard to keep her out of the public eye. To keep her from being hounded just because she's my child. If I choose to lie about how old she is, that's my decision."

"So it's all for her, is it?" he asked, his skepticism clearly visible in the moonlight sifting through the skylight. "Does she know that?"

"It's complicated, all right?" She turned away from him, forcing tired feet up the steps. "I'll talk to her. She'll understand."

"Will she? Because I don't. Why lie about something like that?"

A laugh completely devoid of humor escaped her mouth and she stopped, tipping her face up to the ceiling. "Why lie?" She half-turned on the stairs, meeting his gaze with the hardness in hers. "Because I had the biggest hit of my career when I was seventeen. Because most of my fans still are that age and they want me to be youthful and fun. Because I sing songs about partying and break-ups and people already think I'm *past my prime* so the last thing I need to do is remind them that I'm old enough to have a nine-year-old kid. Mick Jagger can tour until his bones disintegrate from osteoporosis, but I'm *old* at twenty-seven. Why *lie*? Why do you think?"

He watched her, his only movement a muscle twitching in his neck. "So it has nothing to do with protecting her from the press. It's all about making you look younger."

Her shoulders tensed at his tone. "You don't know what it's like."

"Are you kidding me? Do you have any idea how much *damage* you've done? Do you even care? You're a rock star and a millionaire. You may have people you pay to feel sorry for your poor little rich girl problems, but that isn't my job, lady."

"And where exactly in your job description does it say you're supposed to harass me in the middle of the night when I've been flying for days?"

His jaw tensed and he dropped his eyes. "I'm sorry. But I needed to talk to you about Callie. You have no idea how upset she was when she saw that interview."

Now it was Alexa's turn to avert her eyes, feeling sick that she'd taken Victor's stupid advice to try to look like she was still a kid.

"It's Christmas," Elia went on, his voice low. "She really needs you right now. Needs you to show her that she matters."

Callie was the only thing that mattered—and Alexa couldn't seem to stop screwing up. Her stomach roiled and she fought down the feeling. "I don't need a bodyguard to tell me what my daughter needs." She did the best she could, damn it. She hired the best nannies. She worked hard *for Callie*. "Now if you'll excuse me. I have about five hours to sleep before I have to get ready for another premiere tomorrow."

She turned to continue up the stairs, but the bodyguard wasn't done.

"Seriously? Can't you take some time off? Actually see her now that you're back?" he called after her. "It's Christmas."

"I have obligations." Did he think she didn't want time off? That she wasn't exhausted? Did he think this was her *dream*? "I can't let up now. We can't all be Cher. The rest of us are just marking time until we're replaced by the next hot young thing. Every year there's someone younger coming along. I'm only a couple years away from being someone who used to be famous. I have to make this last. This could be my last tour. Without it, I'm just some has-been. Some girl who used to sing doing reality TV in a desperate attempt to cling to fame."

"Maybe you shouldn't be clinging to fame. Maybe you should be clinging to your daughter."

She went still on the stairs. "You don't know me or my life or my daughter."

"*You* don't know your daughter."

The words landed in her stomach—another sickening ingredient to the nauseous cocktail as an emotion she couldn't identify buzzed inside her head like angry bees. "And you do? After one week?"

"I know she deserves better—"

"You don't know us!" she snapped. "And I don't have to listen to this." Who did he think he was? He wasn't even a nanny. Just a bodyguard who thought he knew everything about her daughter after a week. A *week*.

"Alexa." Her name was hard. A command. What right did this man have to command her?

"You're an *employee*, Elia," she snapped, flinging the words at him. "Or you used to be."

That got his attention—the arrogance left his face, wiped away by shock. "What?"

"Your services are no longer required." She swallowed past the knot of anger lodged in her throat. She'd trusted him and he'd been judging her the entire time, lying in wait to accuse her. "Get off my property. If you're still here in fifteen minutes, I'll have you arrested."

Anger flashed on his face, but he controlled it quickly, though his eyes stayed dark. No longer smiling, the Samoan. "Alexa—"

"We're done here, Mr. Aiavao." She continued up the stairs, faster now, trying not to run. She refused to let him run her off. "Stay away from me and my daughter."

"I have to say goodbye—"

That spun her around. "No. You don't have any rights here. This is my house. My child. And you don't get to tell me what's best for her. If you try to talk to her before you leave, I'll make sure Elite Protection can't afford to keep you. Do you like your job, Mr. Aiavao?"

His jaw worked, eyes black in the low light. "I'll go," he conceded. "But you know I'm not wrong about Callie," he couldn't seem to resist adding. "You have to savor every second with her, because you never know when it's going to be taken away."

Her eyes flared wide. "Are you threatening me?"

Something indescribably sad entered his eyes. "No, Ms. Rae, I'm not threatening. Just the voice of experience." He turned back to Callie's wing. "I'll get my things."

Alexa stood on the steps, watching him go, her pulse hammering with some emotion she couldn't identify. When he was out of sight, she hurried up the stairs to her room and pulled up the video feeds on the console beside her bed. There was Callie, sleeping peacefully in her bed, oblivious to what had just happened in the foyer. Thank God.

And there he was, the big, interfering man. In his room. Packing his things. She told herself she was

LIZZIE SHANE

watching to make sure he wasn't stealing anything, but she knew that wasn't it. But still she didn't look away.

He was no one. Just a man who thought he was right about everything—she'd met her fair share of men like that in her life. As if they had a direct line to the secrets of the universe and could pass judgement on everyone else.

Yes, she'd made mistakes over the years, and maybe she shouldn't have said Callie was six on television, but she was doing the best she could. She was doing what was best for Callie. She had to believe that. It was the only way she could keep going.

This was right for them. The work. The long hours. The money. It was the right thing. Callie would forgive her. She would understand. In the long run, she would be grateful.

Which didn't explain why Alexa felt tears pressing up against the backs of her eyes, hot and hard.

Do you have any idea how much damage you've done?

He didn't know her. He didn't know what he was talking about. He'd spent a week making peanut butter and jelly sandwiches for her daughter and suddenly he was the expert? No. She didn't deserve his anger. She didn't.

But even after Elia Aiavao left the house and the sound of his engine retreating down Mulholland had faded in the distance, Alexa couldn't seem to stop reliving his words. They haunted her, pushing sleep away, making her stomach churn, until the small hours of the morning when exhaustion finally won, dragging her under for a few short, restless hours.

He didn't know. He couldn't. Her daughter was happy. She had everything she needed.

Didn't she?

CHAPTER TEN:
TRUTH AND CONSEQUENCES

It was wrong, leaving like this in the middle of the night.

He should have said goodbye, regardless of what Alexa wanted. He'd left a note, because the idea of just vanishing on Callie, when so many things in her life seemed to go up in smoke, made something inside him rebel, but he still felt like he hadn't done enough as he drove down Mulholland as dawn began to break over the horizon. It was later than he'd thought. Or earlier.

He shouldn't have ambushed her like that. Not in the middle of the night. He'd been restless, listening half the night for the sound of Alexa coming home. He should have just let her go to sleep, talked with her calmly in the morning—he'd seen the exhaustion in every line of her body when she'd stood below him in the foyer. He should have kept his damn mouth shut—

But the idea of Callie waking up in the morning and her mother not even being there because she was off getting ready to woo the press at some premiere had dug under his skin, needling at him. The idea of Callie hurting another day, when no days were ever guaranteed, the injustice of Talia being taken away from a family who would kill for another second with her when Alexa couldn't seem to spare even a thought for her child...

He hadn't been thinking clearly.

He'd wanted Alexa Rae to be better than she was—and it had bit him on the ass.

Elia called his boss on his cell thirty minutes before the Elite Protection offices opened, wanting to give his side of the story before Alexa Rae had the chance to make her case.

"Elia. What's up? All good at the Rae compound?" Max answered promptly, but Elia could tell by the sound of his voice that he was distracted. Max was all business when he was at the office, but since his daughter had been born he'd been showing up late to work and walking around with a dopey smile on his face. Cross was taking over some of the administrative duties, but today Elia needed to go straight to the top.

"Actually, she fired me." He didn't try to sugarcoat it or pull his punches.

"She what?" He had Max's full attention now.

"When she got back from her press tour last night, I ambushed her and told her off."

"*You* did?" Disbelief filled the words. Elia's reputation for being unflappable had been well-established.

"I wanted you to know, before she calls you about a replacement or wants to cancel her Elite contract."

"Hold on—what did you say that she was so upset about?"

Elia hesitated, feeling strangely like he was betraying Callie's confidences by talking about her. "She lied about her kid's age in an interview and Callie saw it. I basically told her she should get her head out of her ass and get to know her kid."

A lingering pause met the words as Max absorbed them. "Okay. If she wants a replacement, I'll send Pretty

Boy. He's good with isolated celebrity kids. Thanks for letting me know."

Elia almost didn't want to press his luck, but… "That's it?"

"I should have known it would have been a tough situation for you. All things considered."

They'd never talked about Talia. Elia hadn't realized Max even knew about his niece, but he must have. Candy's background checks didn't leave details like that out.

"I should have handled it better," he admitted. He hadn't been thinking. He'd just wanted Alexa to see that she was wrong. He'd wanted her to change. To suddenly become the mother Callie deserved. It hadn't occurred to him until he was packing his things that he would have been better off keeping his mouth shut so *he* could be there for Callie.

"Yeah, well, hindsight's twenty-twenty," Max commented. "Do you still want to work through the holidays?"

"If you have something for me." He needed the distraction now more than ever.

"I'll see what we have."

Elia signed off, relieved but still feeling the heaviness that had come with the realization that he'd let Callie down. Maybe he could apologize. Maybe he could still fix this.

* * * * *

"What do you mean he isn't here?"

Alexa flinched at the shrill note in Callie's voice. She was sitting in the makeup chair in her powder room, while Margie and Lola fussed with her hair and makeup. The rest of her team orbited around her,

95

everyone focused on their part of making her camera-ready. Callie stood next to one of the large mirrors, her face set into militant lines.

"He's not working for us anymore," Alexa said, trying to move her face as little as possible as Margie dabbed and painted. "Mia is going to stay with you today instead."

Callie's gaze flicked with patented disdain to the assistant before returning to her mother. "I want Elia. When is he coming back?"

"He isn't," Alexa tried to instill soothing calm into her voice, rather than the guilt she felt. When she'd had to explain the situation to Victor this morning, she'd felt incredibly foolish. Yes, Elia had crossed a line, but firing both their bodyguard and nanny on the spot may not have been her best option. Especially because she was too ashamed of the truth in his words to admit to Victor why she'd really fired him.

Her manager had assumed that Elia had made some kind of inappropriate pass and Alexa had let him think that, but now, with Callie glaring at her accusingly, she felt even worse about her impulse decision to throw him out.

"He wouldn't just leave me," Callie insisted. "Elia isn't like that. He isn't like *you*."

Alexa heard someone suck in a breath, but there were too many people in the room for her to identify who exactly had been shocked by the vitriol in her daughter's voice.

"How are we doing?' Victor swanned into the room, then frowned as he seemed to notice the tension vivid in the air. "Are we ready to go?"

"Yes," Alexa announced, rising from the makeup chair whether her face was done or not. The swarm of activity circling around her moved toward the door as everyone gathered up what they would need to keep her looking flawless through all of her appearances today and for the LA premiere tonight.

"No!" Callie shouted, startling Lola into dropping a flattening iron. "I want Elia!"

She flew toward Alexa, her small fists raised, and Alexa caught her arms before she could make contact. "Callie!" She tried for stern, but could hear the panic in her own voice. "I don't have time for this today. You have fun with Mia and we'll discuss it tomorrow."

"No! Now!" Callie yelled. "I want to discuss it *now*."

Victor wrapped his arms around Callie, lifting her off the ground and gently extracting her from her mother's grip. A piece of crumpled paper fell from one small fist and Alexa caught it reflexively. "We can't always get what we want, pet," he said, sympathetic.

"I never get what I want," Callie stated—and the edge of tears in her voice made Alexa blink back tears of her own.

"Go," Victor instructed, nodding Alexa toward the door.

It was back. That helpless horrible mother feeling. The one that never quite left. "I love you, Callie. We'll talk tomorrow."

"I hate you!" Callie shouted back. "You ruin everything. You know what I want for Christmas? To be far away from *you*."

No one gasped this time. The silence in the powder room was echoing. For a long moment no one moved. Then Alexa said, "I'll see you tomorrow," and took a step toward the door and suddenly everyone was moving at once.

She was halfway down the stairs before she thought

to touch her face to make sure she wasn't crying. A little surprised when her fingers came away dry, Alexa glanced over as Lola gently touched her arm.

"Kids say stuff like that all the time. She didn't mean that."

"I know," Alexa murmured back, grateful for the words, though she wasn't sure she believed them.

Maybe Callie really did hate her. And if she did... could she blame her?

Victor was the last one out of the house. As soon as he climbed into the back of the SUV with her, they pulled away, the rest of her entourage in the other car— either to give her space or to gossip about what a horrible failure of a mother she was. Maybe both.

Alexa realized she was still holding the crumpled paper that Callie had been carrying, as they began the winding drive down Mulholland. She smoothed it out, realizing with a jolt that it was a note. From Elia.

Dear Callie,

I'm sorry I won't be staying until Christmas like we talked about. I would stay with you if I could, but sometimes our responsibilities don't let us do what we want to do. I wish I could have stayed to say goodbye, but I will be gone by the time you read this. I hope you have a wonderful Christmas and that you keep believing. I will always be your friend.

Elia

P.S. Your mom really did know how old you were. She was just tricking that talk show host. She loves you more than you know.

Alexa's stomach dropped as she read the note again. He could have thrown her under the bus, could have blamed her for his departure or told Callie the whole truth about the age lie, but he hadn't. She'd made him leave her daughter in the middle of the night and he'd done everything he could to make sure Callie wasn't hurt by his disappearance without making Alexa into the villain.

Why?

"Are you okay?" Victor asked gently.

"Fine," Alexa said, her eyes trained outside at the passing scenery though she saw none of it, the words of the note playing over in her mind.

"Alexa."

"She hates me," Alexa murmured, only able to admit the words because she was alone with Victor in the back of the limo.

"She doesn't hate you. She barely knows you."

The words were gently spoken, but she felt tears trembling on her lashes all the same. The worst part about the truth in what he said was that she didn't know Callie either.

"Hey." Victor handed her his pocket square. "Don't smudge the make-up. Margie will never forgive me if I let you smudge. Her reputation is at stake."

Alexa offered a half-hearted smile, dabbing carefully at the moisture around her eyes.

"You could take some time off after this," Victor offered. "We don't have anything until the tour—just the rehearsals, but I can try to buy you some time to take a break. I know you love working, but you haven't had more than a week off in the last five years. Maybe it would be good for you. Take some time to enjoy what all your hard work brings you."

Alexa grimaced. She'd never been good at that part. Whenever she wasn't working she was always afraid that she wouldn't ever work again. That the universe would discover she'd been given better than she deserved and it would all go up in smoke.

"Don't decide right now," Victor said. "Take a few days. Sort things out with Callie. Spend some quality time."

"I'm not sure she wants to spend time with me."

"Of course she does. You're her mother."

Alexa shot him a look and Victor shrugged in silent acknowledgement of her point. He'd been there from the beginning. He knew she'd never been mother of the year.

She'd been so freaking *scared* when Callie was born. She knew nothing about children—but she knew how the industry worked. And how quickly she would be replaced if she didn't drop the baby weight and get back out on tour without missing a beat. Keep recording. Keep producing. Keep touring.

Her career had been taking off—so she'd been able to afford the best nannies and the best personal trainers to help her with her two singular goals: take the best possible care of her baby and keep making money so she could afford to pay for that care.

Yes, she'd missed the first words and the first steps, but the nannies had sent her videos and she'd told herself that was enough. Callie wouldn't remember that stuff anyway, right? Alexa was the breadwinner—and one with a limited shelf-life. Hot young singers were a dime a dozen, more of them popping up every year on those reality shows. If she didn't keep pushing, she'd be replaced.

Victor had comforted her when she'd cried about someone else teaching her daughter to read, reassuring her that she was making the right decision, that Callie would get opportunities she hadn't been able to dream of when she was a girl.

The mansion she'd bought for them was everything a

little girl could want. The school Callie went to was the best in California by far. The nannies, the tutors, the bodyguards—everything was top of the line for her baby. Which meant top of the line price tags.

So Alexa kept running on the hamster wheel of her life. Performance after performance. Paycheck after paycheck. Song after song. The Princess of Pop. Hardest Working Teenager in the Music Biz.

Mother of the freaking year.

She knew exactly how they'd gotten here. She just didn't have the first idea how to change things.

"Just get through tonight," Victor urged. "Then maybe you can take some time off and get to know your kid."

"That's what we fought about. The bodyguard and I," she admitted. "Callie saw me claim she was six. She thought I really didn't know how old she was. He was pissed at me for upsetting her and I fired him."

"No one blames you—"

"I blame me." She looked at Victor. Always supportive, always calming, always helpful Victor. "Maybe it's about time someone else blamed me too."

Her manager's brow wrinkled as he tried to figure out how to manage her out of her current mood before she had to be sparkling and witty for the television audience.

She was at the heart of an empire, an industry in her own right, but if she didn't want to make a tough decision there was always someone there to make it for her—and then a dozen people to reassure her that she'd done the right thing. Part of her had liked giving that control to Victor. If she wasn't in control, she could pretend it wasn't her fault. But it was. She had no one to blame but herself for how bad things had gotten with

Callie.

She didn't have the first idea how to fix it.

Though maybe she knew somebody who did. Somebody who wouldn't tell her what she wanted to hear, but what she *needed* to hear.

Callie didn't get attached, but she'd gotten attached to him. Why? Alexa didn't trust easily, but she'd trusted him—not just to take care of Callie, but not to hate *her*, to give her the benefit of the doubt, to tell her it was all okay. And when he'd told her the truth instead, she'd thrown him out. But now...

"Maybe I will take a few days off," she said to Victor. "But first—could you get an address for me? There's something I need to do."

CHAPTER ELEVEN:
BLACK TIE APOLOGIA

Elia would have been less surprised to be served with a restraining order than to have a Grammy-winner in a red carpet gown ring his doorbell at five o'clock that afternoon. She looked like a fifties starlet fantasy, but her eyes were serious. Intent. And glittering with remorse.

"I'm sorry for the way I behaved last night. Can we talk?" she asked, nodding past him to indicate she'd like to come in.

After a long moment, Elia collected his jaw off the floor and stepped back to let her past him. "Sure. Of course."

She moved into his apartment with a waft of perfume and rustle of expensive fabric. He closed the door and turned to face her. His apartment was small—a single open concept kitchen/dining/living room with a master bedroom and bath to one side. It was a bit of a mess, but she didn't seem to notice the dishes in the sink or the half-read books scattered on the coffee table as she turned to him, smoothing her hands over the luscious silver fabric hugging her hips.

"You look..." There were no words in the English language adequate to describe her.

She glanced down at her dress with a little frown, as if she'd forgotten she was wearing it. "Sorry. I know it's a bit much. We were on our way to the premiere when Victor got your address and since you live so close to the theatre I wanted to stop on the way. Sorry to drop in on you like this."

That was three times she'd apologized. An act he wouldn't have thought the great Alexa Rae was capable of five minutes ago. "Is Callie all right?"

"She misses you." A slight pause. "And she hates me." Alexa choked up on the second sentence, the words filled with emotion that she somehow kept from falling from her eyes and ruining her makeup.

"She wouldn't watch your interviews if she hated you." Callie obviously still cared for her mother. Or at least was fascinated by her.

Alexa swallowed, visibly trying to bring herself under control. "I didn't know she did that. I don't know a lot of things about her, to be honest. You were right. Everything you said last night, I deserved."

"My timing could have been better. And my delivery. I know I was out of line—"

"Don't apologize," she cut him off before he could. "People don't tell me things like that. They tell me what I want to hear, but I think I needed to hear the truth. Even if I hated it at the time." She grimaced delicately. "I hate it now, but I hate the fact that it's true more than being told."

He nodded, unsure where she was going with this, waiting for her to tell him.

"Do you think you could come back? For Callie...and for me?"

He hesitated—not because he wasn't sure he wanted to go back for Callie, but because he wanted to so badly the sharpness of that desire startled and unnerved him.

"I know I said I didn't owe you an explanation,"

Alexa went on when he didn't immediately respond, "but I feel like you deserve one."

He shook his head. "You don't have to—"

"No. I do. When Callie was born, I was so scared. I'd always wanted to be a singer. A star. I didn't know what it meant, but I wanted it so badly and it felt like I was right on the brink—I could make myself a name or I could vanish into obscurity, just another one hit wonder. If I wanted a career, I had to drop the baby weight and be a sex symbol again as fast as possible. I knew nothing about being a mother, and I was so scared of screwing up. Screwing *her* up. I didn't know what to do. I barely remembered my mother. My father... Victor had gotten him into rehab, but I didn't trust him anywhere near a baby. Dare was gone and I had to get back on the road. Everyone said so. My career wouldn't be there waiting for me if I took a few years off to be a mom. And what kind of mom would I be? An eighteen-year-old kid with a GED who used to be famous? I didn't know what to do, so Victor brought in the best nannies and wet nurses in the world and they took care of everything. Callie would cry whenever I held her and I felt like such a failure as a mother, but on stage I knew what I was doing. I was filling arenas. I was killing it. And I was happy there, but I felt guilty all the time because I liked being at work better than I liked being at home. But then I was nominated for my first Grammy and I was headlining an arena tour and everything seemed to be taking off—but only if I could go with it. Only if I was willing to put my career first. So I did. And I don't know if I made the right choice. Everyone told me I did."

She grimaced. "How do you know? When you're famous, every blow is softened for you. Everything that's hard or bothersome is taken care of for you. I don't have to drive myself anywhere or do my own taxes or go grocery shopping. Or take care of my kid." She grimaced bitterly. "Being a parent is hard, and I have dozens of people who exist to make the hard things just go away. So someone hires the perfect nanny and I only have to see my daughter at prearranged times, like some kind of British aristocrat."

Alexa shook her head helplessly. "I didn't set out to be that kind of parent, but I never knew how to be any kind of parent at all. I still don't." Her eyes met his. "But I'd like to learn. Somehow you managed to make my daughter care more about you in a week than I managed in her entire life. How did you do that?"

Elia looked at the glamorous pop star standing in his kitchen, seeing instead the woman whose lower lip trembled. "I listened," he said simply. "I spent time with her. I made sure she knew that she was my priority."

Alexa sniffed, wrinkling her nose. "I'm not sure she wants to spend time with me."

"She might not admit it, but I think she does. You could try getting away from the entourage for a change. I've been talking to her about Christmas wishes and she said she'd like to see snow. You could get away. Just the two of you. Tahoe, maybe," he said, remembering where the snow-making machine research had taken him.

"Could you come too?"

"For security?"

The words gave her an easy out, but she shook her head, her eyes vulnerable. "I don't know how to be alone with her. Could you teach me? Please?"

He hadn't wanted to spend Christmas with a family. He hadn't wanted to be around children or any of the holiday trimmings. But Elia Aiavao had never been able to resist a damsel in distress, and apparently he still hadn't developed that skill.

"Okay," he heard himself agreeing, the word somehow distant as something about this woman wormed its way past his defenses. Just like her daughter had. "Let's go to Tahoe."

* * * * *

"Elia! You're back!"

Alexa tried to ignore the bite of jealousy as her daughter raced across the foyer and flung herself against the bodyguard's legs. He patted Callie gently on the back, some emotion she couldn't identify passing over his face. Something much more complicated than simple happiness at seeing Callie again.

Was he thinking of his niece?

She'd seen the photos in his apartment yesterday. The place had been small and very male, obviously the home of a bachelor, but there had been framed photos of Elia smiling as he held a little girl along with a few scattered pictures of the same little girl with a beautiful dark-haired woman she assumed was his sister.

Callie pulled back, glowering up at him—and Alexa was marginally relieved that she wasn't the only one who'd ever been on the receiving end of one of Callie's death glares. "You left without saying goodbye."

"I'm sorry. That was very bad of me," he agreed. "But you know how it is for Santa leading up to Christmas. You never know when I'm going to have to rush up to the North Pole to deal with a rogue reindeer."

Her eyes narrowed even further. "You aren't Santa."

"Are you sure you don't believe me even a little? Even if I tell you that we're going to go see snow?"

"We are?" Interest lit her eyes, the glare falling away—and Alexa experienced another stab of jealousy, this time that Elia had been the one to tell her.

"I thought we could take a trip," Alexa interjected, feeling like an imposter in the conversation when they both looked over at her. "Just the three of us." She swallowed past the thickness of her nerves. "Would you like that, Callie?"

"Lake Tahoe has some of the best skiing in the state," Elia added. "You've never seen so much snow."

"Really?" But Callie wasn't looking at him, or asking about the snow, she was frowning at Alexa, as if unsure she should trust the offer. "We're really going somewhere together?"

"Really," Alexa promised, pushing a smile past her guilt. Why hadn't she thought of this years ago? Could it really be this simple to put that hopeful light into her daughter's eyes? "We thought we'd drive up there today. Would you like that?"

Callie's expression closed off as she visibly restrained her hope, giving an apathetic shrug. "I guess."

"You guess?" Elia asked with mock horror. "Snowball fights and snow man building and ice skating and you just *guess*?"

Callie cracked a tiny smile at the exaggerated faces he was pulling. "Okay, it could be fun."

"Of course it will be! Do you need help packing all your warm things?"

"I can do it," Callie insisted, already turning and rushing back toward her wing.

Elia turned to her, the smile he'd worn for Callie slow to fade from his face. "How about you?" he asked. "Are you ready for this?"

She couldn't remember the last time she'd been this nervous—ten thousand screaming fans weren't this scary—but she nodded, forcing a smile. "Absolutely."

CHAPTER TWELVE:
WHITE CHRISTMAS SNAFU

In retrospect, they really should have checked the forecast in Tahoe.

After a seven hour drive during which Callie spent the majority of the time jacked into her tablet and Alexa tried not to feel awkward riding shotgun beside a man who didn't seem to know the meaning of the word awkward, Elia pulled the SUV to a stop in the driveway of the chalet Victor had arranged for them.

The sun was setting over the mountains, casting them in a golden light, which would have been gorgeous and inspiring, if not for the fact that they were very *green* mountains.

Alexa had frantically searched the internet on her phone as they approached their destination with no noticeable whitening of their surroundings and had discovered two things. First—that Tahoe only experienced a white Christmas about once every three or four years. And second—that Tahoe had been experiencing an unusually warm December which had made it impossible for the ski resorts to even manufacture snow.

She felt like an idiot. She felt like she'd lied to her daughter. And she wanted to smack the mountain of muscle in the driver's seat for even suggesting a plan that was so obviously doomed to failure—especially when he cut the engine and turned to them with a bright smile.

"Here we are!" he announced with irritating cheer.

Callie looked out the window, her skepticism taking on levels of scorn Alexa hadn't expected to encounter until the teenage years. "More snow than I've ever seen? Nice one, Santa."

"Callie—" Alexa started to scold, but Elia was already responding.

"Hey. Don't underestimate the Claus," he insisted, so visibly unbothered by their lack of wintery surroundings that Alexa found her aggravation growing in direct proportion to his calm. This was supposed to be the perfect Christmas getaway. How could it be that if they started off by lying about snow and couldn't do any of the winter games he'd promised?

Elia hopped out of the car, heading to the back to get their bags and Alexa twisted in her seat. "Why don't we see what the house is like? Might as well make the best of things."

Callie rolled her eyes, saying nothing, and climbed out of the car after Elia.

"Great," Alexa muttered. Trying to muster up some enthusiasm, she stepped out of the SUV and walked to the rear, where Elia was handing Callie her suitcase.

"Why don't you go check out your room and get settled? Maybe later we'll order pizza and watch *White Christmas*—that's a movie where they don't have any snow either. Then you can help us figure out what kinds of stuff we need to stock up on at the store tomorrow. I'm thinking marshmallows and jellybeans for every meal."

Callie rolled her eyes—at least Alexa wasn't the only

one getting that treatment—and turned to trudge toward the house, dragging her bag.

Alexa watched her go, a pit digging deeper and deeper into her stomach. If she didn't have an ulcer by the end of the weekend, it would be a minor miracle. "There isn't any snow," she hissed as soon as Callie was out of earshot.

"Hey." Elia grinned, repeating, "Don't underestimate the Claus. There's a snow machine at the resort. They'll have snow."

"It's sixty degrees. They can't even make snow in this weather." She'd Googled it.

"Then we'll just have to improvise." His constant good mood was going to give her a nervous breakdown. "Cheer up, Alexa. She didn't really come for the snow."

With that he turned and headed up the walk—on his way to intercept Callie who had stopped at the front door, stymied by the keypad lock for which Victor had given Elia the code.

Elia evidently thought Callie had come along for the quality family time, but Alexa couldn't quite convince herself that her child actually wanted to spend time with her. Especially when Callie had already vanished into her room by the time Alexa made her way up the front walk and into the chalet.

The A-frame home had a rustic charm—exposed beams and a giant fireplace dominated the two story great room. There was a loft above and a hallway leading toward what she assumed must be the bedrooms. A granite breakfast bar separated the kitchen from the great room and a gorgeous floral arrangement sat on the counter.

Alexa shrugged out of her coat, hanging it on the rack for outerwear beside the front door, and toed off her boots, padding in her socks to investigate the flowers. The note tucked in among the blooms had an A scrawled across the front. When she flipped it open, the message was brief and to the point. *Enjoy yourself. Love, Victor*.

If only it were that easy.

A quick survey of the kitchen showed that it had been fully stocked, every detail thought of. Trust Victor to make sure she had everything from creamer to celery on her impromptu getaway.

"Looks like we won't need to stock up in the morning after all."

Alexa jumped, shutting the refrigerator abruptly and spinning toward the sound of that deep voice. Elia leaned against the counter at the far side of the kitchen. The space was massive, but suddenly it felt much smaller. Everything about him was so *large*. Even his smile.

"Victor takes good care of me," she murmured, unaccountably flustered.

"I thought the idea was no entourage. Live like normal people."

Alexa blushed, embarrassed that her people had taken care of everything. "We can still order pizza and watch *White Christmas*."

Elia smiled—and that smile alone seemed to scream that everything came so damn easily to him. "I've made it my mission to expand Callie's Christmas movie repertoire. We've been on quite a binge. So far she seems to like *Home Alone* the best."

Alexa wrinkled her nose at her daughter's questionable taste.

"What? Didn't you like movies like that when you were a kid?"

She shrugged. She didn't often think about her childhood if she could avoid it. "I didn't watch movies much." She must have when she was really small. She vaguely remembered Peter Pan and the Grinch, but after her mother died her father hadn't exactly kept it together and movies had only happened during the rare periods when he could keep a job—before he'd go on another bender, get fired, and the cable would get shut off.

"You okay?" Elia must have read something on her face because his voice was sober, his eyes compassionate.

She looked away, toward the back of the house where Callie had vanished. "Of course."

She wanted to ask him if he really thought this trip would do any good, if he really thought things between her and Callie could be fixed, but she was scared of what he would say, scared he would lie to make her feel better and she would know he was lying.

"You really should work on your own movie education since you're a movie star now."

Alexa grimaced, relieved to be back on solid ground. "I'm no movie star. They wanted my voice and were willing to put up with my complete lack of acting chops to get it."

"I think you're a better actress than you give yourself credit for."

"What's that supposed to mean?" she asked sharply, her shoulders tightening.

"You're a performer. When you're on stage, putting on a show, aren't you playing a part? Isn't that acting?"

"That's..." Words failed her as she tried to explain. "That's just being *on*. It's not playing a part. It's the music. Letting it take over until it doesn't even feel like me anymore. I'm just the vessel. Does that make sense?"

Dark eyes studied her. "Do you like it?"

"I..." She frowned. "Of course I do. Why would I do it if I didn't love it? I love my life." And if she sounded defensive it was just because... Because...

"You're lucky. To do something you love."

She latched onto his words. "Did you love fighting? I saw the articles people wrote after your accident. You were famous, at the top of your game—"

"It was an adjustment," he said with a wry smile. As if that was all it was. As if he hadn't lost a leg and his career and everything he'd dreamed for his future. She couldn't imagine smiling about something like that.

"I can't—" She broke off, shaking her head. "How do you smile about that?"

"You think I ought to be railing at the universe?"

"It would make more sense."

"Yeah, but I've been there. Done that. Didn't make me feel any better." He folded his arms and her gaze caught on the tattoos, the strength on display. He was so *strong* and so sure of himself. How did he do that? "Right after the accident, it was rough, I'm not gonna lie. Things changed without my permission, my life took a turn I never would have chosen and yeah, I got angry about it. The unfairness of it. But I had support. My family. A good prosthesist. A good support group. You get through it. And you start living again. My niece thought I was Iron Man." His smile faded for a moment and he swallowed. "I still have phantom pain sometimes, but I got off the pain killers and my life isn't that different. I was always an optimist and I got that back—I survived. We can't all say that."

She knew he was thinking about his niece and part of her wanted to ask what had happened to her, but the words didn't come. Instead she swallowed and said, "It must have been hard, getting off the pills. I don't mess with that stuff. My father... he's been in and out of rehab so many times. I know so many artists who use—something to get them up to perform, something to slow them down so they can sleep—you know it's killing you and you just keep doing it because you need it—" She broke off and Elia's eyes were soft with sympathy.

"Like your husband?" he asked softly.

* * * * *

Elia expected her to dodge the question—he knew he was brushing up against a sensitive subject, but Alexa surprised him, shaking her head and saying, "Dare and I were never married."

His attention sharpened at her words, though he didn't betray it by the twitch of a single muscle. He'd thought she might have been haunted by the pain of her ex's memory, that maybe it was why she was so guarded, so distant, but she spoke of him with a wry, almost bitter twist of her lips.

"Dare wasn't really the marrying kind." She looked up, as if she could see him. "He was in bed with a groupie the night he died, did you know that?"

"I didn't," Elia admitted softly, not wanting to break the moment.

"I was so mad at him for overdosing, but not for cheating. Our life back then...it was too much. They expect you to be something, so you give it to them, because they can get ugly when you aren't what they want, but it's harder than you think it'll be. Harder than you ever imagine. Not that I'm complaining. I *wanted* it. I wanted it so badly. And then I became famous overnight when I was fifteen because a song I recorded myself in this janky little studio became the song of the summer. My dad and I never had much, and suddenly there was money everywhere and he was drinking and doing drugs, in and out of rehab." She swallowed, her eyes distant. "I was overwhelmed and my dad was useless and there was Dare, headlining my first ever tour. The *star*. He was only nineteen, but he'd been famous for years already and he seemed to understand the world I was suddenly a part of. So of course I fell in love with him. He was cynical and funny and moody and unreliable, but I *needed* him. I was totally reliant on him. I'd emancipated when I was seventeen—while I was touring with Dare and riding the success of my one big hit, and I thought I was an adult. I thought I knew what I was doing, but it wasn't a *healthy* relationship. I can see that now. Though I did love him and I think he loved me too. It was hard to know with Dare."

She grimaced, and Elia knew she was no longer seeing the kitchen. "He didn't want kids. Told me to 'take care of it' when I got pregnant. Told me I'd be destroying my career. Wasting my life." She shook her head. "I didn't know what I wanted. I was so confused, and then I met Victor. I was supposed to be touring. I wasn't supposed to be a mom, but he told me it was my choice and he'd help me. Whatever I wanted to do, he'd help me. And right then I knew I wanted her. I wrote songs about it. Half my second album is about falling in love with Callie before she was even born. Then Dare ODed and it came out that I was pregnant with his kid and the paparazzi went nuts. I still don't know if my second album sold because of Dare or because of the music, but it seemed like I blinked and I had a baby I didn't know what to do with—what the hell did I know about being a parent? And my music was going crazy and I needed to tour, but I couldn't have Callie on the road—not with the way I'd seen tours could be. I had to keep her safe, you know? Protected. So I bought her a house and got her a nanny and did what I had to do. But that meant I never saw her and I never felt like her mother. And when I came home from tour I was so tired. I never took sleeping pills or even the 'herbal supplements' that half the pop stars I know take to give themselves the energy to perform. I was so scared of turning into my father. Or Dare. But sometimes it was too much. Just too—" She broke off, sighing. "Too much. And whenever I tried to spend time with Callie, I always felt like I did the wrong thing. I didn't know the baby's routine like her nanny did. I didn't know *her*. And then she was a toddler and a little girl—and suddenly she was old enough to hate me."

"She doesn't hate you."

"No? I certainly hate myself sometimes."

"Don't be so hard on yourself. You want to learn how to be a better mom. That's a start."

"I never wanted to make Callie feel like she was alone. Like she wasn't good enough somehow. I know about that feeling. I've been trying to feel good enough my entire life." She looked at him, seeing him again and her eyes darkened as color drained from her face. "I can't believe I just told you that. Please don't— I don't know why I—"

"Hey," he interrupted gently, taking a step toward her, catching her hand. "You can trust me."

CHAPTER THIRTEEN:
TRUST FALLS

Alexa stared into his dark eyes, the sudden spike of panic slowly abating. She didn't know why, but she felt like she *could* trust him. This man who had somehow earned her daughter's trust as well.

"I barely know you," she whispered, feeling the rough strength of his hand holding hers.

He met her gaze. "You know me."

She couldn't look away, everything in her focusing on his eyes—until a creak down the hallway made her flinch, looking toward the sound, expecting to see Callie, but there was no one there. She pulled her hand away. "I don't—I don't talk about that stuff. Dare. My father. You must be some kind of hypnotist or something."

He stepped back, smiling, letting her lighten the mood. "I have one of those faces. People love to confess things to me."

Her eyebrows arched skeptically. "You do *not* have one of those faces."

"Are you calling me ugly?"

Her gaze traced the lines of his face and her mouth went dry all over again. There was something about him so strong, so masculine. Even his bone structure made her feel safe. How crazy was that? It should have been unnerving—all that strength. He could break her with his pinky finger. But she only felt comforted by him. So incredibly safe.

"Do you do it on purpose?" she asked. "Do you consciously work at making yourself nonthreatening because you're such a physical force?"

An easy smile curled his lips. "And if I do?"

"You're very good at it."

"Thank you." She felt like there was subtext to the words, but she wasn't sure what either of them were saying. "You're a great actor too."

She grimaced, wrinkling her nose. "I'm not."

"Why did you do the movie if you didn't want to be an actress?"

She shrugged. "Victor's trying to turn me into a triple threat. Extend my career any way he can."

"Is that what you want?"

The simple question caught her off guard and she opened her mouth, at a loss for words. She couldn't remember the last time she'd thought about what she wanted. Only what she had to do. Always what she had to do. "I don't know," she admitted, after a long pause. "I want to avoid screwing things up with Callie. If that's even possible."

"You need to stop beating yourself up for the past and start thinking about what you can do in the future."

"Like it's that easy?"

He shrugged. "It's a start. No one gets a handbook when they have a kid. You just have to figure it out. Fake it till you make it."

"But if I screw up—"

"Then you screw up. And she knows you tried."

"I don't even know where to start."

He grinned. "How about with *White Christmas* and pizza?"

"Elia..." It wasn't as easy as that. You didn't just decide to be a good mother and *poof* all problems were solved, all the baggage gone, all the history erased.

"Trust me," he murmured, and he grinned, making everything easy with a curve of his lips—just like he always did—and Alexa nodded. There wasn't anything else she could do.

* * * * *

Alexa barely saw *White Christmas*—though she knew it was wonderful. She barely tasted the pizza—though she knew it was delicious. She couldn't seem to think about anything other than Callie and whether Callie was having a good time and whether this whole week would actually do any good.

Her awkwardness was palpable, but Elia sprawled bonelessly on the great room sectional, as if the idea of tension was a foreign concept to him. She caught him rubbing idly at his thigh once and had to remind herself that he had a prosthesis and maybe it was bothering him. It was so easy for her to forget that he'd lost a limb. He seemed to be one of those people who just adapted, smiling, to everything life threw at him. She was so *jealous* of that.

Callie slumped against his elbow. She'd been using his shoulder as a pillow, but sometime during the last half hour of the movie she'd slid down his arm, scrunching into a knot on the couch. Elia had insisted that she brush her teeth and put on her pajamas before they started the movie and Alexa now saw the wisdom in that. All they had to do was carry her to her room and slip her into bed if she fell asleep.

The foresight spoke of experience—and again she wanted to ask him about his niece. His sister. And why he wasn't with them this Christmas. But for all that he'd told her about himself, his work, and his accident, something about him always closed off when the topic of his niece came up—and she was scared of alienating the one man who seemed to have solved the puzzle of Callie.

As the credits rolled after the last song, he started to move, shifting Callie gently off his arm and setting his feet on the floor, preparing to scoop her up, and Alexa scrambled off the couch in a rush.

"I'll get her," she volunteered.

Elia looked up, startled by the offer. "Are you sure? She isn't light."

"No. I've got this." Callie wasn't awake to push her away—these were the only times she actually felt like she had a right to act like a mother.

She gathered Callie up, staggering a little and Elia braced a hand on the small of her back to steady her. Alexa ignored the alarming heat of his palm—the man was a furnace—and adjusted her hold on her daughter, finding a comfortable position for the boneless heap in her arms. Callie was heavier than the last time she'd done this. It was rare she had the chance to be close to her daughter without the fear that she would do something wrong, say something wrong, and Callie would push her away—this time forever.

She carried her down the hall to the smaller of the downstairs bedrooms. Elia had claimed the pull-out in the open loft area above the great room, leaving Alexa the master next to Callie's room, but he followed her down the hall now, holding Callie's door open for her so she could maneuver through the doorway without bashing herself or her daughter against the frame.

Callie didn't even sigh as Alexa set her gently down

on the bed and tugged the covers over her. She smoothed the hair back from her daughter's forehead, trying to ignore the ache in her chest. How had she let things get so bad between them? Was there any way back? Would this really do any good? She was terrified of failing, but she had to try.

Alexa moved to the door, where Elia waited. He flipped off the light, leaving the door cracked so the light from the hall trickled in.

She was steps away from her own door, but instead of retreating she hovered nervously in the hallway. Elia glanced at her, lifting his eyebrows in silent question.

"Are you sure this is a good idea?" she whispered. "Do you really think it will make a difference?"

"I think she wants a way to get through to you as badly as you want one to get through to her. You need to show her she can believe in you."

"What if she doesn't forgive me? For all the times I haven't been there?" Alexa asked, her most pressing fear coming out before she could think to filter her thoughts.

"Then you keep being there for her until she does." He said it like it was simple. And for someone like him, maybe it was. He was so strong. So resilient. There was physical proof on his body of what he'd been through in life, but he kept smiling. How did he do that?

"I don't think I'm as strong as you are."

As soon as she said it, she realized how stupid it came out, but Elia seemed to know what she meant. He seemed to see through the physical comparison of their sizes to her underlying fear that she'd let it get to this point because she was a weak person, always taking the path of least resistance. Letting other people arrange her life for her in ways that took away all the hard choices so she never had to be strong enough to make them.

"You wanna know a secret?" he asked. "No one starts out strong. Strength—in all its forms—comes from repetition. You work your way up. Don't try to bench press your weight right away—practice with the little weights first. Focus on the little things—like tucking her in—and the big things will come in time. And whenever you're afraid you can't do something, just think about the fact that you don't want to be that weak person and let that fuel you to be stronger."

"You make it sound so easy."

He shook his head, his ever-present smile muted. "Hardest thing in the world. But you'll get there. You're tougher than you think."

She didn't know who he saw when he looked at her, but she liked the idea of being the person he saw. What had he said earlier? Fake it until you make it? Could she pretend to be strong until she built up her strength?

For Callie, she would try.

She looked up at him in the golden light of the hallway, this man who seemed to break everything down and make it seem so simple. Who made things seem possible rather than helplessly beyond her reach. How did he do that?

"Thank you," she whispered, her gaze catching on the firm line of his jaw, the soft curve of his lower lip.

"All part of the job," he said with a grin, lightening the mood right when a strange pressure began to press against her lungs. "I like helping people. Even if those people are spoiled diva pop stars who don't know how to grocery shop anymore."

"It isn't that I don't know *how*. I shopped for my dad and me all the time when I was younger." Half the time he wouldn't be able to do it himself. "It's just different now. Everyone knows my face. I think the last time I was in a grocery store was when I was dating Dare. It was before I was really famous, but we were recognized and all of a sudden there was this mob of people surrounding us. He loved it. Encouraged it. But I'd never felt so overwhelmed. We didn't have security with us and it took us an hour to get from the checkout to the door." She shrugged. "When that's grocery shopping, it's easier to just send someone else to get your milk and orange juice."

His smile faded. "I didn't mean—"

"I know." Her life didn't have a whole lot of normal in it, but maybe that was what this week could be. A chance to have a little slice of normal with Callie and this man. She flushed, glancing behind her toward the master suite. "I should go...get some sleep."

He nodded. "Good night."

She swallowed thickly, backing toward her room, feeling unaccountably warm. "Good night, Elia."

* * * * *

Elia watched Alexa walk away, silently reminding himself of all the reasons he shouldn't get involved with her. She was a client. And not just any client. She was Alexa Rae, a woman who couldn't even go grocery shopping without being mobbed.

And then there was Callie.

She had to be the priority right now. Even if he seemed to have developed an acute, inappropriate awareness of her mother. Alexa was gorgeous, yes. And undeniably sexy. But it wasn't the Pop Princess persona that attracted him. It was the woman he saw underneath—barely daring to hope, so uncertain, but with something unbreakable about her that made her vulnerability that much more compelling.

But no matter how compelling she was, the last thing Callie needed was to think he was only using her to try to get close to her mother. No. Even if Alexa were interested—which he had no reason to think she was—that wasn't why he was here.

His phone rang as he was checking the locks and the cameras he'd set up earlier. He glanced at the screen, frowning at his sister's name. She was still trying to get him to come home for Christmas, but he knew he was doing the right thing. He knew what she was trying to do—bring them together, convince them that they could still make happy memories and be a family without Talia—but she also knew him too well to believe fake smiles, and they would be fake. Christmas was too hard. The memories still too raw. Sefina was trying to move on and he wanted that for her so badly, but having him there when he couldn't be strong for her would only add to her stress and her sadness. No. It was better this way.

The call went to voicemail and he pocketed the phone without listening to the message, telling himself again that he was making the right choice.

Being here. Doing something good. That was all he could do.

Tomorrow they would commence Operation Happy Christmas, but tonight everything was quiet. An idyllic little getaway with a rock star who didn't seem to like being a rock star very much and her daughter who didn't seem very comfortable just being a kid. Both of whom seemed to have snuck beneath his defenses when he wasn't looking.

He wasn't shy about talking about his past, but he never talked about Talia—and he'd almost done that today.

She'd been the difference, after his accident. When

he'd been frustrated and angry and in pain, she'd never stopped seeing him as a superhero. She'd been the reason to fight to get better. The reason to keep smiling. To keep laughing. To remember the good and not let the things he couldn't control define him.

He'd be a different man today if not for her. But then she'd been taken away. So fast and so damn unfair and he wasn't ready to try to make memories without her. He wasn't ready to stop being angry about the fact that she wouldn't have any more Christmases—even if he covered it with smiles. Two years wasn't enough to forgive the universe for taking her away.

So here he was, hiding from his sister at Christmas, and falling for another little girl and her mother.

Elia scrubbed a hand down his face. God, he hoped he knew what he was doing.

CHAPTER FOURTEEN:
BANANA PANCAKES & OTHER ADVENTURES

Elia had second thoughts about the big happy Christmas plan the second he walked into the kitchen the following morning and saw the look of unhinged panic on Alexa's face. She stood over a smoking skillet, frowning intently at something that might have been pancake batter in another life.

"What's cooking?" he asked, taking a cautious breath and finding the aroma surprisingly appealing.

"Banana pancakes. I hope." She frowned at the batter. "Callie isn't up yet and I remembered one of our cooks saying this was her favorite, so I found a recipe online, but I haven't really gotten the hang of the flipping yet."

He came around the island, examining the blobs of half-cooked batter piled on a plate to one side that hadn't made the transition to pancakes.

"Here. It's all in the wrist." He reached around her, putting his hand over hers on the spatula and showing her how to gently scooch it beneath the circles and flip in one smooth motion.

Or he tried to. She resisted his attempt to guide her and they ended up with another lumpy half-flipped blob.

He chuckled as she made a frustrated noise. "Let's

try that again." He braced his free hand on her hip—purely platonically, just to guide her—and felt her go rigid under his grip, but the distraction was enough that she let him flip without interference and they wound up with a perfectly symmetrical pancake. "Voila."

"Is there anything you aren't good at?" she grumbled, as his hand over hers flipped another pancake.

"Nope," he said cheerfully. Though he wasn't so certain she'd still be singing his praises at the end of the day.

Yes, she'd asked for his help, but what did he really know about kids? Maybe the whole bonding plan would backfire terribly and they'd be even worse off than before. What right did he have to teach Alexa how to be a mom? He'd gotten through life on confidence and charm, but this was a kid he was messing with. She deserved better than his amateur attempts at child psychology. And so did her mother.

Alexa, who wanted so badly to do the right thing and was so scared of screwing it up. And who felt entirely too good beneath his hands.

Elia handed her the spatula and stepped back. "Now you try."

She attempted another pancake flip—and managed to flip it into a reasonably symmetrical shape. "I did it!"

She turned to him, her face radiant with joy—and her smile knocked the breath out of him. *This* was Alexa Rae. When she glowed like that, it was easy to see the star. No wonder she was blindingly famous. Helen of Troy had nothing on her.

He was in so much trouble.

"Elia?" Her smile faded when he stared too long and he cranked up the wattage on his own smile to cover the lapse.

"Congratulations. First step, pancakes. Second step, world domination."

She giggled, the sound indescribably sexy, and Elia was hit again with the stakes of what he was playing at today. Alexa and Callie were both so vulnerable, both reaching for love and fearing they would never find it. If he could just get the two of them to see how much they already cared for one another—

"What are you doing?"

At the sound of Callie's voice, Alexa's smile froze in place, her hand clenching on the spatula. He was tempted to step in, to smile, to smooth things over, but this was the first test and he wanted to see how she reacted. *Come on, Alexa. Fake it till you make it.*

* * * * *

Alexa felt Elia looking at her, urging her to respond as fear of saying the wrong thing filled her mouth with sawdust. It was so much easier to think of what to say to her daughter when she didn't have the girl standing right in front of her, a minefield of prickly reactions.

Elia lifted his brows encouragingly and his words over the last few days echoed in her thoughts. *Fake it until you make it. Focus on the little things. Let the fact that you don't want to be weak fuel you to be stronger.*

She *didn't* want to be weak. She wanted to be the kind of mom Callie could rely on.

Gripping the spatula hard, Alexa squared her shoulders and swallowed down her fear. She loved her daughter like crazy—and she could play the part of the loving mom who didn't have almost a decade of guilt weighing her down. A woman who was confident that her love would be accepted by her daughter because she'd never done anything to deserve rejection. A woman who knew how to talk to her daughter and just did it.

She grabbed onto the part with both hands and half-turned toward Callie with a grin. "Making breakfast!" she announced cheerfully. "Banana pancakes with chocolate chips and whipped cream on top."

"Really?" Callie came over to investigate, her expression dubiously optimistic.

You and me both, kid.

"It smells good," Callie said—more than a little surprise in the words.

"Hopefully it tastes as good as it smells. I tried a new recipe I found online." She reached over on impulse, giving Callie a sideways squeeze around the shoulders, releasing her before she could pull away. "Why don't you set the table? Maybe Elia can help you find the silverware."

Callie and Elia exchanged a glance and moved to do as she asked. Maybe she was laying it on a little thick, but the words pouring out of her mouth comforted her—and if she was talking she wasn't second-guessing. Much.

"I thought maybe we could go look for a Christmas tree today," she announced cheerfully as she plated her most successful batch of pancakes. "If we're going to be here until Christmas, we'll need all the trimmings. There has to be a Christmas tree lot around here somewhere, even if they don't have snow."

"Are we really staying until Christmas?" Callie asked and Alexa couldn't quite read her tone.

"Would you like that?" she asked, turning away from the stove with both hands full of plates and suddenly Elia was there, taking two of them from her and carrying them to the table in the breakfast nook. "We rented the place for the week."

Christmas was only four days away. The idea had been to come up to Tahoe for the weekend, but when Victor told her he'd booked the place through the twenty-seventh the idea of staying through Christmas had taken hold. They hadn't decorated the house in LA yet. They might as well stay up here, spend the days decorating and getting ready for the holiday.

Alexa carried the last plates, joining Callie and Elia at the table. She glanced at the bodyguard as she took her seat. "You probably want to be with your family for the holiday," she said to him. "Do you need to get back to LA?"

He shook his head. "I knew when I took the job that it involved working through the holidays."

Callie frowned at the pair of them and Alexa flashed a smile she hoped didn't look fake as she placed her napkin in her lap. "Dig in," she encouraged—hoping the pancakes were edible. She'd meticulously followed the directions, but she hadn't turned on a stove in years, let alone attempted an actual recipe.

She watched nervously as Callie and Elia cut into the pancakes, holding her breath as they took their first bites. Elia's eyebrows lifted in surprise and Callie's furrowed in what could have been irritation or confusion. "They're *good*," she announced.

"Really?" Alexa couldn't keep the surprised hope out of her voice as she took a bite of her own—and tasted the surprisingly delicious combination of flavors. "Well, what do you know? I can cook."

Elia laughed. "Don't act so surprised. Just pretend it all came out exactly as you planned. That's the secret."

"Of course it did," Alexa said, with blithe confidence

so overblown Callie giggled. Alexa smiled—a little spark of wonder unfurling in her chest. She'd actually made Callie giggle. Her daughter was smiling. Laughing. Having fun *with her,* not in spite of her. Maybe this could actually work. Hope expanded to fill the gaps in her confidence. "What do you say, Callie? Should we get a tree today?"

"That could be fun," Callie conceded, and Alexa felt another little spark of victory.

She met Elia's eyes across the table and smiled. She didn't want to get ahead of herself, but if they could just have one perfect Christmas, that was something, wasn't it? They could build on that.

This could work. This could really work. Suddenly she didn't feel quite so hopeless.

* * * * *

The GPS indicated they were still ten miles away from the tree farm Elia had Googled when traffic on the country road suddenly slowed to a standstill. The rock star in the passenger seat sat forward, frowning at the line of cars as if they had been dropped in their path for the express purpose of frustrating her.

"Is it an accident?" Alexa demanded, craning her neck, but Elia had already spotted the source of the slow down.

"It's a Christmas fair." He pointed off to the left. "Look."

Alexa frowned in the direction he'd pointed. Ever since the pancake episode, she'd been in manic Christmas mode—trying so hard it made him tired just looking at her, but he couldn't fault her enthusiasm, even if it did seem more than a little desperate and Callie had definitely sensed the desperation, though she was going along with it for now.

"A fair?" Callie's curiosity wafted up from the backseat. "Like with rides?"

"And reindeer, by the look of things." He could see tents, stages, and, yes, the infamous holiday livestock. Alexa was frowning—a fair wasn't on the agenda she'd mapped out, but in Elia's experience the best memories couldn't be planned. "What do you say, ladies? Detour?"

"Really?" The squeak of hope in Callie's voice decided him, but he looked to Alexa and lifted one eyebrow.

"We're going to need to get decorations for the tree somewhere and I think I see a few ornament booths," he commented.

Alexa looked uncertain—which he was starting to find was her natural state, but she put on a smile. "I think we need to check out this Christmas fair. See if it's up to Santa's standards."

"He isn't Santa," Callie groaned from the backseat, but her pre-teen drama queen act evaporated in the next second as Elia turned into the parking lot for the Christmas fair. He could see her in the rearview mirror, her gaze hungrily taking in every detail. She might try to play aloof, but Callie was enchanted.

Elia parked the car and Callie launched herself out of it like she'd been shot from a cannon. Alexa scrambled out, trying to keep up. "Callie, stay close," she called, and Callie rolled her eyes at the restriction, but she didn't try to rush ahead as they approached the fair.

Booths and tents selling every sort of Christmas decoration imaginable had been set up in a rough semi-circle inside a second larger semi-circle of food and drink stands. A small livestock pen to one side held a pair of reindeer while a second corral offered pony rides. Near the reindeer—but upwind—a small stage had been set up where an incredibly authentic looking Santa merrily ho-ho-hoed and took photos with kids who'd come to tell him what they wanted for Christmas. Another stage stood empty, but by the look of the matching outfits of the kids mingling behind it, it would be used for performances before long.

On the opposite side of the fair there were larger tents, which upon closer inspection they discovered had been heated and chilled respectively for gingerbread house building and ice sculpting competitions. The largest tent was also chilled and contained a small oval ice-skating rink.

Elia scanned their surroundings, looking for security risks, but though several people did double takes when they saw Alexa, no one approached them.

They strolled through the fair, checking out the various vendors. To the outside observer, they may have looked like any normal family, but Elia couldn't help noticing the way Alexa kept trying to engage Callie and the girl kept subtly shooting her down.

"What do you think of these, Callie?" Alexa pointed to a set of beautiful, hand-painted Christmas ornaments. "Aren't they pretty?"

Callie shrugged, barely glancing at the ornaments. "I guess."

"Maybe something else," Alexa conceded, smiling to the vendor who had been gazing at her worshipfully since they walked into the shop, though Alexa didn't seem to realize she'd been recognized, her attention focused on her daughter. "How about the sparkly ones?"

Callie gave a half-hearted jerk of her shoulder this

time.

"Why don't we start with stockings and come back to ornaments?" Elia suggested, coaxing them out of the booth. At the next stand, he left Alexa talking to the vendor about embroidery to personalize the stockings, tugging Callie to the far side and crouching down in front of her, carefully balancing his weight. "Okay, what's going on?"

Callie shrugged one shoulder, looking away, and for a second he thought she would stonewall, but then she grumbled, "She's being weird."

"Weird how?"

"Pretending she likes me and stuff."

Oh sweetheart. His heart broke, but he just braced her shoulders gently between his hands. "I don't think she's pretending. Your mom loves you like crazy. She's just learning how to show you."

Her jaw jutted out. "That doesn't make sense."

"It's like…math." Confusion had Callie furrowing her brow, puzzled out of her pout, and he knew she was listening as he went on. "I'm lousy at math. I always *wanted* to be able to solve the problems, but I didn't know how. I tried a bunch of stuff that didn't work, stuff that only made the problems harder, and then eventually someone taught me a way that made sense and I could do math. It was never natural for me. You know? Your mom…she loves you so much, but no one had ever taught her how to show it. She didn't know how to take care of you, so she hired people who were *amazing* at math to help you, but now she's trying to learn herself, does that make sense?" Callie shrugged in reply, but her eyes were pensive. "So maybe give her a chance? She may not be very good at it yet, but she's your mom. Yours. And that counts for something."

Callie glanced down, but he could tell she was considering it so he decided to settle for that. He stood and they rejoined Alexa, who was holding two stockings—one red and traditional and one white with so much glitter it could probably be seen from space. Callie jutted her chin toward the glitterbomb. "That one's nice."

Alexa's relief that Callie actually liked something was almost painful to look at. "Great! Shall we get it? Do you want to help me pick out some for me and Elia?"

Callie gave a half-shrug and Alexa beamed like she'd been told Santa was real and he was on his way. They dove into the piles of handmade stockings and Elia stood back to give them some room. When Alexa managed to coax a smile from Callie, her own smile could have lit up an entire power grid.

Damn, she was gorgeous. Even without a drop of makeup and no stylist in sight, she still had something that made everyone in her vicinity want to gather around her like gathering around a campfire on a cold night.

She'd tugged on a dark blue cap earlier, joking about going incognito, but even before she'd absently removed her sunglasses, everyone had known who she was. She *glowed*. People couldn't miss that.

He couldn't miss that. No matter how much he might want to, for self-preservation.

Alexa and Callie approached the vendor—and Elia saw a flash of panic cross Alexa's face. He was at her side before he was conscious of moving. "What's wrong?"

She leaned toward him, turning her body away from the vendor so they wouldn't be overheard. "I don't carry money," she whispered. "I haven't paid for anything myself in years."

A blush rode her cheeks, which was entirely too adorable—though he needed to not think of his client as adorable. Elia pulled out his wallet. "I'll expense it." He spoke over her head to the clerk. "Do you take credit?"

The vendor, who looked so blown away by having Alexa Rae in his booth he probably would have given her the stockings for free, nodded enthusiastically. "We take everything."

Alexa whispered, "Thank you," tucking her arm through his—and he tried not to revel in the feel of her against him. She was a job—and Callie came first. Even if Alexa was starting to burrow into his heart alongside her daughter. He was a professional. He could handle this. Eyes open, hands off.

CHAPTER FIFTEEN:
COCOA & OTHER TEMPTATIONS

The Christmas fair was a godsend.

Alexa had been nervous at first—going into all those people, taking Callie with her into a situation where they could be mobbed—but Elia was there. She knew he would look after Callie. And after her.

And ultimately, no one had bothered them. She hadn't even caught anyone trying to sneak a picture, though she had a feeling more people recognized her than let on. It was sweet of them really, the vendors and fair patrons going along with her tacit request for privacy. She could feel Elia scanning the crowd at her side, but instead of making her paranoid, it just made her feel safe.

Everything about him made her feel safe.

They bought ornaments, stockings, garland, and even a Santa hat for Elia—which had made Callie roll her eyes, but Alexa could tell her daughter was fighting a grin. Callie was having fun. With her. She wouldn't have believed it was possible two weeks ago.

They shared a makeshift lunch of pretzels and roasted chestnuts as they strolled the aisles. Callie was dubious about the spinning carnival rides, but couldn't seem to get enough of the reindeer. And somewhere between the pony rides—which she declared herself too old for—and the ferris wheel—which she declared "unstable looking", she started to relax and just be a little girl enjoying a day at a Christmas fair.

Alexa felt her own smile becoming more relaxed, more natural and less surprised every time Callie's seriousness cracked into a smile.

After visiting the reindeer for the third time, Callie tugged them over to the skating rink, eyeing it covetously. "Can we go?"

"You two can go. I'll watch from the sidelines," Elia said before Alexa could agree for all of them—she'd been agreeing to everything, afraid to say no, but now she glanced at Elia, remembering his leg and the fact that balancing on blades might be more complicated for him.

Callie looked up at him, something moving across her expression before she nodded decisively. "I don't want to go either."

Elia smiled at the quick reversal. "I appreciate the solidarity, but just because I can't do something doesn't mean you should deny yourself something you like."

"What's solidarity?"

He glanced to Alexa for support, but she just lifted one eyebrow in a *go on, you got yourself into this* gesture that made him grin all over again. "Solidarity is when you do something or don't do something to support another person. When you want to stand with them."

Callie nodded, mulling that over. "Okay. I'm solidarity with you. Can we see Santa now?"

"Sure," he agreed, and Callie rushed off to join the line, leaving Alexa to trail behind with Elia. "Sorry I can't skate," he murmured as they followed.

"It's okay. I don't know how to skate anyway," Alexa confessed, keeping her tone light. "And I'm pretty sure

I'm not supposed to do things like that. My body is insured. If I break my leg on the ice, it screws up tour schedules."

"Callie says you tour a lot. Do you go out again soon?"

"January," she admitted, hating the reminder of the life that was waiting for her back in the real world.

She'd been loving this day, feeling like this little Christmas fair and the Tahoe chalet were a pocket outside of time where the normal rules didn't apply. Where she didn't have to be Alexa Rae and be on all the time.

She stepped closer to him to allow a harried mother herding four children to pass and Elia moved closer, shielding her from the crowd with his bulk. They reached the Santa line, where Callie already stood, and found a place to wait for her outside of the main pathway's traffic.

"Do you still love it?" he asked. She glanced up at him and he clarified, "Performing. Touring. All of it."

"I…" It was on the tip of her tongue to say *of course she did*. Habit. Automatic. "I do," she said finally, but her gaze landed on Callie and the weight of all she gave up by being on tour settled in her stomach. "My mom taught me to play the guitar so long ago I barely remember it, and I used to dream about filling stadiums. The screaming fans. Back when I was too young to think about the rest of it. To understand everything that came with it. The pressure to keep performing, keep producing, stay on top." She shook her head at the girl she'd been. "It felt like a fantasy when it happened. People cheering for *me*. That feeling of holding thousands of people in the palm of your hand. Nothing had ever made me feel like that. Like I was good. Like I was special. But then you get off stage and you second guess it. You doubt yourself. And you want to get back out there and feel it again to convince yourself it wasn't a fluke. Or a dream. It's this crazy ride. This out-of-body experience. Having Callie made it real. And scared me shitless." She grimaced. "I still love it, but I'm so *tired* all the time. It's too much, but if you slow down, even for a second...what if it all goes away?"

"Then you find something else to take its place."

She looked up at him, shaking her head. "You always make it sound so easy."

"Does it have to be hard? Do you need to keep pushing? Keep touring? At some point don't you get to enjoy what you've worked for?"

Alexa gazed up at him, the words somehow baffling. When was the last time she'd just *enjoyed* what she'd earned. Was it possible that she never had? Because she never felt like she'd earned it. She always felt like she had to keep running. The hamster on the wheel. "I don't know how to slow down," she admitted.

"So you learn." They both watched as Callie climbed up on the stage and approached Santa. "You're already proving you can."

Feeling her face flush at what felt like a compliment, Alexa pulled out her phone, lifting it in camera mode to capture what appeared to be Callie's interrogation of Santa Claus. The girl didn't go easy on anyone.

"I don't know who I'll be if I'm not performing anymore," she admitted, "but it's only a matter of time. Sometimes I look at my old press clippings and all I can think is, *God, look how young I was*. I look in the mirror and know it's all downhill from here."

"Stop it. You're more beautiful now than you've ever been."

LIZZIE SHANE

Alexa looked up at him, startled, the cell phone frozen in the air—and saw color rise to Elia's cheeks. He hadn't meant to say that.

She flushed, focusing back on the cell phone, pretending she wasn't suddenly short of breath. How did he do that? Make her feel so special with a single impatient sentence? Make her feel like she was more than her market value?

She shouldn't be falling for him. Even if he was incredibly sexy. Even if he was strong and gorgeous and made her feel safe and special and like she could actually *do* something about all the helpless corners of her life.

He was her bodyguard. And he was also her link to her daughter. She needed to keep a safe distance.

But she was glad he didn't take it back.

"He's a *much* better Santa than you," Callie announced as she bounded off the stage, shattering the strange, fragile moment suspended between Alexa and the bodyguard. "His beard is *real*."

Elia put on an easy smile for Callie, swinging her around. "I told you, my beard is invisible because I have so much magic."

Callie arched a skeptical brow, smirking. "Uh-huh. Sure it is."

Elia glanced up at Alexa, catching her smiling, and his own smile seemed to shift, growing easier. "Cocoa?"

"You read my mind."

Elia adjusted his one-handed grip on their shopping bags and herded Callie toward the cocoa stand, Alexa falling in beside him. Where there had been only awkwardness this morning, everything felt so natural now. So easy.

Callie sipped her cocoa, giggling when she got

whipped cream on her nose and Alexa self-consciously dabbed at the cream that clung to her upper lip—

And caught Elia watching her, unsmiling, his gaze fixed on her mouth. She blushed, looking pointedly at her cup, staring into the hot chocolate, suddenly breathless. When she dared look up again, he was scanning the crowd.

A children's choir had taken the stage, soprano voices singing about hearing angels on high, and they stopped to listen. Elia lifted Callie up on his shoulders so she could see over the crowd and caught Alexa's hand, tugging her close against his side—and she went breathless all over again. She stared blindly at the stage, pointedly not looking at the man at her side until several seconds had passed, then she allowed herself to glance down to where their fingers were linked.

He'd only pulled her close for security reasons. So she couldn't be pulled from his side. She told herself that. But his hand felt good. His strength felt good. Everything about him felt good. And this moment...this moment felt amazing.

Maybe she was only falling for him because of what he was doing for her and Callie. Because of who he was, and how she felt when she was with him, and how incredibly sexy he was with muscles on top of muscles...

Okay. Bad line of thinking.

Why ever she was falling for him, she needed to stop. That wasn't what this Christmas was. She couldn't get mixed up with Elia. This Christmas had to be about Callie. And it had to be perfect.

CHAPTER SIXTEEN:
TIMBER

By the time they left the Christmas fair, picked out the *very best* tree at the Christmas tree lot and drove back to the chalet, Elia was starting to feel as if he'd been flattened by a semi, but Callie somehow still had the energy to chatter merrily away in the backseat, laying out her plan for baking Christmas cookies for Santa. Something had changed today. The little girl who was too jaded and worldly to believe was now throwing herself into Christmas. It would have warmed his heart if he hadn't been so tired.

He didn't delude himself that their work was done, that everything would be smooth sailing from here on out, but at the moment Callie was smiling, Alexa was smiling. And if that was a minor Christmas miracle, he would take it.

Gravel crunched under the tires as he pulled up in front of the chalet and Alexa sighed, sounding almost as worn out as he felt. But even exhausted, with the mother of all headaches throbbing behind his eyelids, he still didn't want the day to end any more than Callie did.

It had been a damn good day.

The sun was already setting, though it was barely five, and Elia had already seen how quickly it could get dark in the mountains. "Why don't you two go in and see what you can scrounge up for dinner while I take care of the tree?" he suggested. He didn't want to wrestle with getting the thing off the roof of the SUV in the dark. His neck already ached with borrowed tension just thinking about wrangling ten feet of uncooperative fir.

"Are you sure you don't want help?" Alexa offered.

"You'd only be in the way. Go in and get warm." The weather had turned while they were at the Christmas tree lot and though it wasn't cold enough to threaten snow, the forty degree drizzle seemed to seep through his coat and saturate his bones with an aching chill. "No reason for all of us to be miserable."

Alexa shot him a look, but didn't argue as they all climbed out of the SUV. "Callie, would you help me with the bags?" When her daughter was occupied with their purchases, Alexa rounded the SUV to Elia's side, lowering her voice. "Are you okay?"

"I'm great. It's just been a long day." He turned to cough into his shoulder and when he turned back Alexa was frowning. "I'm *fine*. Go inside. The sooner you get out of my way, the sooner I can get the tree inside."

Her frown didn't abate, but she went, albeit slowly. "Let me know if I can help."

Elia wrestled with the straps securing the tree to the roof of the SUV with hands that suddenly felt stiff and thick-fingered. His headache throbbed—a louder beat in his brain with every second he was out in the drizzle that slithered down his neck with icy fingers.

He'd loved the tree when they spotted it on the lot, full and green and towering above the others—mostly loving the way Callie's face had lit up when she saw it— but by the time he maneuvered the damn thing off the roof and up to the front porch, he was starting to wish

Callie had fallen in love with a smaller tree.

Callie must have been watching for him because as soon as he approached the front door it opened and Callie held it wide, bouncing with excitement as he manhandled the tree through the opening, staggering a little under the weight.

"Elia?"

He ignored the concern in Alexa's voice, carrying the tree over to where she and Callie had set up the tree stand they'd bought. Alexa was completely inept when it came to helping him position the base of the tree in the stand and securing it, but he managed not to curse at anyone as they tried again, and again, and—finally victoriously—a third time to get the tree straight in the stand.

They stood back, admiring their work. It was like something out of a Christmas commercial, massive and majestic—and listing ever so slightly to the left.

"Do you think we got enough lights?" Alexa asked. The tree lot had sold strands of lights, but the tree looked much bigger in the house than it had outdoors. Even with the two story ceilings in the great room, it dominated the space.

"We're gonna need a ladder to decorate it," Callie announced, sounding delighted.

"I think I saw a step stool in the pantry," Alexa commented—the words seeming to come to him through a tunnel of static.

How did they have the energy to even *talk* about decorating it? Didn't they feel as flattened by the day as he did?

"Elia?" Alexa's voice was miles away, though he could see her in front of him, her hand rising to his face.

"I'm fine," he grunted.

Her hand was icy on his cheek. "You're burning up."

"I am?" As if her words gave him permission to be sick, the world went into a flat spin and everything about the way he'd been feeling for the last hour suddenly made sense.

"Why didn't you say you weren't feeling well?"

"I'm fine."

Alexa made a low, frustrated sound. "You're swaying on your feet. Men are such idiots about getting sick," she grumbled. "Come on." She tucked herself under his arm and began guiding him...somewhere. He wasn't aware of where they were going, only of Callie's worried face swimming in his vision. Alexa seemed to notice her daughter's concern at the same moment. "Callie, can you look for a medicine cabinet for me? See if we have any Advil or Tylenol?"

Callie darted off and Alexa huffed under his arm as they trudged down the hall. It wasn't until she shoved him onto a bed that he realized where they were. "This is your room." He tried to stand up and she shoved him back down.

"You're barely mobile. There's no way I'm trying to get you up to the loft. If you fell on those stairs, you'd take me down with you and that's not how I want to die." She gave his shoulders a single shove and he fell back onto the bed, proving he wasn't so much with the stability at the moment. "I'll sleep on the pull out. You sleep here."

"Not exactly how I was hoping to get into your bed," he muttered.

* * * * *

Alexa froze at his words, but Elia's eyes were closed. He obviously had no idea what he was saying. Delirium.

That was all that was. The man was feverish. His eyes had been downright glassy when she'd finally wised up and realized why the Smiling Samoan was no longer smiling.

She wrestled off one boot—the man's foot was the size of Mount Everest—and frowned at the other, unsure if she should remove his prosthesis. It seemed like an incredibly personal thing to do, but he'd be more comfortable sleeping without it, wouldn't he? Though she wasn't sure she could get at it without removing his jeans and she was pretty sure she couldn't wrestle him out of them without more cooperation.

Alexa put her hand on his forehead, concerned by the heat—and how quickly this had come on.

"I found this," Callie announced from the doorway, holding up a medicine bottle.

"Good girl." Alexa rose, putting up a hand to forestall Callie when she would have entered. "Don't come in, sweetie. I don't want you getting sick too."

Callie frowned, handing over the bottle. "Is he okay?"

"You bet," Alexa said with more confidence than she felt. "This is just like when you got the flu in September. It seemed bad at the time, but it was over before you knew it."

Callie's brow wrinkled in a frown, but she didn't argue.

"Why don't you see if there's any soup in the pantry?" Alexa suggested—hoping the task would be a welcome distraction for her daughter as it would have been for her. She always preferred to be doing something. Even if it wasn't much. "Soup is always good when you're sick."

Callie nodded and retreated, leaving Alexa with Elia

passed out on the bed.

She checked the bottle, reading that one of the things it did was reduce fevers—thank God—and wondering what his other symptoms were. Until he woke up, she was flying blind. She pulled out her phone and Googled what to do for a fever. The internet didn't seem to think fevers were a big deal unless they were accompanied by other symptoms or the fever was dangerously high, but without a thermometer how was she supposed to tell? Why didn't phones come with thermometer apps?

She found one article recommending cold compresses and several advising fluids. Okay. She'd get him a glass of water for when he woke up. Or should she wake him to take some Ibuprofen and take his temperature?

She missed Victor keenly—Victor who would just swoop in and take care of things. Call the doctor if he needed calling, bring in nurses if he needed nursing. They'd agreed no entourage, but surely Callie would understand if Alexa called in the cavalry now. Or would that be cheating? Elia was sick—but he was sleeping soundly, not thrashing around like a deathbed scene in a movie, so maybe he was okay? Maybe it was nothing worse than a nasty cold?

Alexa reined in her panic and retreated to the kitchen for the water—finding Callie neatly lining up rows of soup cans on the countertop.

"These are our options," Callie declared as soon as she noticed her mother. "I think Chicken Noodle is best, but if we run out of that we have Chicken with Rice and Chicken with Dumplings. I don't know what Italian Wedding is."

She was so serious. So focused on her task. So determined to make Elia better by categorizing their soup options. And Alexa's heart melted into a puddle of goo.

She crossed the kitchen, pulling her daughter into a hug—and for once Callie didn't stiffen and pull away. She leaned into Alexa's embrace, tucking her head down. "He's going to be fine," Alexa reassured her, finding comfort in her own words and the feel of Callie's small arms wrapped around her middle. "You're a great kid, you know that?" she said. "I don't deserve someone as amazing as you."

Callie pulled away then, her brows tugging into a frown. "How did you know I was sick in September?"

"I always know what's going on with you," she said—hoping it sounded more maternal and less Big Brother than it did in her head. "When Pilar said you were sick, I got on a flight to come home, but I was in Prague and before I was even halfway back we heard you were better already. Hopefully Elia will get well just as quickly."

Callie turned back to the row of soups. "Which one do you think he would like best?"

CHAPTER SEVENTEEN:
FLORENCE NIGHTINGALE, ROCK STAR EDITION

Elia groaned as he came awake, reluctant to open his eyes even though the throbbing headache seemed to have temporarily moved on to torment someone else. But when he did dare to crack his eyelids, the sight that greeted him made it worth the effort.

Alexa lay curled on the armchair beside the bed, one arm tucked under her head while the other dangled toward the floor. A damp blue washcloth lay on the carpet beneath her hand, where it must have dropped when she fell asleep. Elia had vague memories of that cloth pressing against his neck and forehead, the cool relief of it like heaven. With that memory came others—Alexa helping him out of his jeans and removing his leg, leaning over him, urging him to drink or swallow something. A thermometer being shoved in his mouth. Chicken soup.

She was quite a nurse, this rock star.

He didn't know if he made some noise or if she sensed him watching her, but she stretched in the chair and opened her eyes, meeting his gaze steadily. "Hey."

There was something intimate about knowing how she woke up. That she didn't blink sleepily and cling to sleep, but instead simply opened her eyes—from sleep to awake with no in between. "Hey," he replied, through a throat that felt like shattered glass.

"You're looking better," she said, rising from the chair and collecting the dropped washcloth, setting it on a bedside table he could see was littered with the debris of the last night—pill bottles and half-empty glasses and bowls.

"I still feel like hammered shit," he grumbled, trying to swallow through the pain in his throat. She touched his forehead and he realized what an ass he was being. "Sorry."

She shrugged. "I wondered if you would ever stop smiling. Guess all it takes is a mild case of plague." She pulled back her hand. "At least your fever seems to be gone. You had us worried."

He glanced toward the door, but it was closed. "Callie?"

"She made you soup. Then I sent her to bed with a promise that if you needed anything I would wake her up. She's very attached to you, you know."

He was attached to her too. Far more than he should be if he knew what was good for him.

A cough rattled his chest and brought him half-upright in bed. Alexa tried to give him a glass of water but he fell back to the pillows with a groan. "I hate being sick."

"Really? And most people enjoy it so much."

He slanted her a look. "Smartass." He would not have pegged the aloof Alexa Rae as a wiseass, but she gave him a little smile as she tidied up the mess on the bedside table.

"I'm just glad to see you doing better. Who knew the big strong man would be brought low by the sniffles."

This didn't feel like the sniffles. It felt more like the

plague she'd joked about, but he didn't want to scratch his throat any more by arguing.

"Can I get you anything?" she asked. "Tea with honey?"

He'd never been a tea guy, but that sounded better than just about anything on the planet. He nodded. "You're good at this," he whispered, since whispering didn't hurt his throat.

"Fake it till you make it," she said cheerfully. "I don't have the first idea what I'm doing. Thank God for Google." She hitched up the dishes in her arms and turned toward the door. "I'll be right back with that tea."

He didn't think he closed his eyes for more than a second, but he must have dozed off because when he opened his eyes again she was there at the bedside again, holding a steaming cup. She glanced at him apologetically. "Sorry. I was trying not to wake you. I'll just set the tea here and you can have it when you're up to it."

"No. I'm up," he scratched out, propping himself up. She helped him adjust his pillows and he found himself saying again, "You really are good at this. Good instincts."

She grimaced, stepping back once he had a good grip on the cup. "It's all Google. I don't know what I'm doing," she repeated.

"No one knows what they're doing. I think all parents are just faking their way through the best they can. Scared out of their minds of screwing up half the time."

"That sounds like the voice of experience."

"My niece," he admitted. "Talia." Saying her name didn't hurt as much anymore, but it still made something in his chest pull tight.

Alexa nodded, and he could have left it there. She wasn't going to push it. But something prompted him to explain.

"My sister and I were raised by a single mom. We were always close—twins—and I wanted her to know she could always rely on me. Her husband—he's a nice guy, but he traveled a lot for work so when someone needed to take Sefina to a doctor's appointment when she was pregnant, she called me. My mom moved to Hawaii a few years ago, so when Talia was born and Sefina needed help with the baby, I was there. I know Talia wasn't mine, but I loved her more than I'd thought it was possible to love another human. She made everything better, made it magical—and when I had my accident, she was the reason to fight to walk again. This little girl...she saved me." The words made it hard to breathe, so Elia focused on inhaling the scent of the tea.

"What happened?" Alexa whispered—and Elia met her eyes.

"She died."

* * * * *

Alexa felt guilty for pressing him as soon as she saw the look on his face, stark with loss. The Smiling Samoan hid a lot of very real emotion behind his smile. It was easy to assume he was shallow with his easygoing manner, but she'd known there was more—she just hadn't expected seeing it to make her feel so raw.

"You don't have to—" she began, but he shook his head.

"It's okay. I just don't talk about it." He met her gaze, grimacing. "Leukemia."

Alexa swallowed against the sudden press of tears, remembering vividly his words from the night she'd fired him. *You have to savor every second with her, because you never know when it's going to be taken away.*

"It happened so damned fast. One day she's this healthy, happy kid and the next..." He shook his head. "We tried every treatment out there—I went bankrupt to pay for anything that might help, but in the end nothing did."

"I'm so sorry," Alexa whispered, the words beyond inadequate. How did he keep smiling? How did the weight of something like that not crush him?

"I was a wreck when we lost her," he admitted. "I had a hard time being around Sefina. We both found it too painful to remember. We're talking again now, but over the holidays...it's harder. I barely remember last Christmas." His smile was heartbreakingly sad. "Talia loved the holidays."

"You should be with your family," she whispered.

"No. Sefina keeps inviting me, but I would only make it harder for everyone if I was there. I took this job over Christmas so we could pretend we were spending the holidays apart out of necessity and not because we can barely look at each other."

Alexa swallowed, sure she was going to say the wrong thing. "I'm sure your sister would want you with her, but I'm selfishly glad you're here. Grateful for everything you've done for me and Callie."

"You two are more similar than you think. You can be a good mom, Alexa, if you give yourself the chance."

His eyelids drooped and Alexa stepped in to take the mug away from him before he could spill the tea. "I'll let you get some rest."

It was a testament to how exhausted he was that he didn't protest, sliding down on the pillows and closing his eyes before she even left the room.

Alexa tried to work the kinks out of her spine as she moved down the hall toward the kitchen, but the crick in her neck felt like it had been welded in. Sleeping in the chair hadn't been the best idea she'd ever had—especially after Elia's fever broke and it became apparent he was not, in fact, going to need to be rushed to the hospital for an emergency appendectomy or whatever they did for people with viral meningitis.

WebMD had not been her friend.

She could have gone to the loft and flopped on the pull out, but it was so far away and she'd wanted to be able to hear him if he should relapse and call out to her. Yes, maybe she'd overreacted—it certainly seemed that way in the light of morning when a flicker of a smile was already trying to return to his face—but she wasn't good at this real life stuff and she would have been too worried to sleep if she'd gone upstairs.

The bed was king sized—she probably wouldn't have disturbed him if she'd curled up on the far corner of it, but the memory of the way he'd said he wanted to get her into bed stopped her. Not that he was in any shape to do anything. Not because she was scared he would actually try something—but because it scared her how much she wanted him to.

She hadn't had anything resembling a romantic relationship in a long time. People described her as beautiful and desirable in TV intros and magazine articles, but the closest she'd come to feeling like someone actually wanted her in the last few years was the love scene in the movie.

And, despite what the magic of Hollywood would have its viewers believe, filming that scene was far from romantic. Hard to have a sense of intimacy with twenty people moving around you trying to make sure your face caught the light and your nose wasn't shiny.

But still, that scene, where someone was looking at her like she was a treasure, that scene was the closest she'd come to that feeling. But this wasn't an illusion. This wasn't the safety of the set. This was someone real. Who seemed to really want her. And that was terrifying.

"How is he?"

Alexa looked up from the open pantry she realized she'd been standing in front of for the last five minutes, staring blindly at the rows of cereal with thoughts of Elia racing through her mind. Callie walked over to the breakfast bar and climbed onto one of the stools, looking like her night had been about as restful as Alexa's.

How had this man come to mean so much to her in such a short time? So much to both of them?

"He's doing a lot better," Alexa reassured her. "His fever is down, but he's still tired. He'll probably sleep a lot today."

Callie's forehead wrinkled. "Fever is one of the first symptoms of encephalitis. And ebola."

"Okay, no more internet for either of us," Alexa announced, swiping Callie's tablet off the breakfast bar and moving it to the far counter with her phone. "Elia is going to be just fine. He caught a bug, but he's doing better already. What we need is something to distract us, so we don't spend all day hovering over him and making him crazy while he's trying to sleep." Her gaze caught on the giant—ever so slightly listing—tree in the great room. "What if we decorated the tree to surprise him?"

Callie's brow puckered again in concentration. "Do you think he would like that?"

"I don't know, but I've been asking myself: What would Santa do?"

Her daughter rolled her eyes. "He isn't Santa."

"I know he isn't *the* Santa, but he's kind of been our Santa. Do you think you could help me do this for him?"

Callie thought it over for a moment before giving a decisive nod. "We're going to need tinsel."

CHAPTER EIGHTEEN:
DECORATION DICTATOR

"Higher on the left. Right there! Just like that!"

Alexa stood on her tiptoes on a chair, her arms stretched above her head as she attempted to hang a strand of garland over the window while Callie stood back and called directions. It turned out her daughter was something of a dictator when it came to decorations—and Alexa was loving every second of it.

She'd been nervous at first, scared that without the buffer of Elia—who had still been sleeping every time they'd checked on him—their relationship would regress back to the arctic chill of before, but she and Callie had discovered a shared obsession for making the Christmas decorations *perfect* and things had been... well, if not perfect, then at least pretty damn amazing.

Alexa had figured out how to use the stereo—with only a small amount of assistance from her tech-savvy daughter—and put on a Christmas channel that played softly in the background as they trimmed the tree and decked the halls. From time to time, she would find herself singing along to the familiar melodies and she thought she even heard Callie humming at one point, though she never sang the lyrics.

Did she not know them? Alexa tried to remember if she and Callie had ever sung Christmas carols together.

Those first few Christmases had been work, work and more work—and telling herself that Callie was too young for Christmas to mean anything yet. By the time she realized she was missing something, the pattern had been established. In more recent years, she'd started inviting her daughter to do things with her and being turned down, leaving Callie to her own devices, not wanting to force it, until Christmas became a pile of gifts and an awkward dinner with Callie and Victor.

Had she ever sung with her daughter? Her own memories of her mother's voice sometimes felt like all she had of her—what did Callie have of her?

"Right there!" Callie coached, and Alexa fished herself out of the memory. She pinned the garland in place with the makeshift fastener and stepped off the chair to survey her work, but as soon as she dropped her arms, the left side sagged and Callie groaned. "It's horrible."

"It has character," Alexa insisted—in part because she wasn't eager to climb back up on the chair and take another whack at it. Her daughter, she had learned, was just as much of a perfectionist as she was, and Alexa's arms were aching from all the decorations she'd held above her head until they were positioned *precisely* as Callie wanted.

Callie was frowning at the offending garland in a way that demonstrated in no uncertain terms that Alexa *would* be getting back up on that chair and fixing the damn thing—she still couldn't bring herself to say no to her daughter, so incredibly grateful that Callie was speaking to her at all—and she was relieved when the sound of her cell phone ringing from the kitchen gave her an excuse to delay the next rep of her involuntary arm workout.

"I should get that."

Callie continued to frown at the lopsided garland as *Jingle Bell Rock* bounced on the stereo and Alexa retreated to the kitchen to grab her phone. Victor's name filled the screen and she smiled, wishing he was here, not so he could fix everything for her, but just so he could see how well she was doing.

"Guess what I'm doing?" she asked him by way of greeting.

"Going to a Christmas fair with your daughter and a bodyguard?"

The light, bubbly feeling that had carried her into the kitchen vanished. "Oh no. There are pictures?"

"Just on social media, and so far we've gotten them to take down any of them that show Callie's face. You're fine. It looked like you were having fun."

"We were. But we'll be more careful next time we go out. Thank you for the warning."

"That isn't actually why I called." There was something in his voice. Something that made nerves twist in Alexa's gut.

"What's wrong?"

"Nothing's wrong," Victor soothed. "It's your father."

The nerves evaporated, vanishing into something hard. "We talked about this."

"It's Christmas. He keeps insisting he just wants to see you and Callie."

"He just wants money or—I don't know what he wants, but I don't care. I don't want to see my father. I don't care if it's Christmas."

A slight pause. "He says he's clean."

"And how long will that last? *No*, Victor. I don't want my father around me and I definitely don't want him around Callie—" She turned, looking back toward the great room to check on Callie—and found her daughter standing at the edge of the kitchen, watching her. "Victor, I've gotta go. We'll talk later."

She ended the call, cursing silently, and trying to replay the conversation, attempting to recall if her daughter would have overhead anything she shouldn't. She didn't talk to her daughter about the human trainwreck that was her father.

"Should we work on that garland?" she asked with overdone cheer, herding Callie back into the great room, but her daughter stopped beside the chair Alexa had been standing on and frowned at her.

She braced for the conversation she could see coming, the questions she wasn't prepared to answer. The guilt and the blame. Her father had always had problems, but he'd kept it under control—mostly—until she hit it big and their world changed.

She remembered her shock when she'd learned there was nothing left of the income from her first album, that her father had somehow spent it all when she wasn't looking. She'd begun emancipation proceedings. She'd put him in rehab. She'd felt like it was all somehow her fault—and so of course she'd given him another chance. And another. Until Callie was born and she couldn't do it anymore.

She was braced for any question—except the soft one Callie asked, "Is he bad?"

Alexa sank down onto the couch, her defenses wilting. "He isn't bad," she admitted. "He's just…" *Weak*. But that wasn't quite right either. "Do you know what an addict is?"

"Someone who does drugs."

"Those drugs, sometimes they change you and you

seem like a different person when you're sober, but then when you start using again, you change."

"And your dad is like that."

Your dad was too. Alexa stopped herself from saying the words. She was always so careful not to speak badly about Dare in front of Callie. Instead she simply nodded.

"He wants to meet me?"

Alexa's lungs seized at the soft question. "He does," she admitted, "but I don't..." She swallowed, trying to find the right words inside her panic. Callie wanted a family, but her grandfather was the last person she needed. "I have to protect you." She shook her head, struggling for words. "I used to let him back in, every time he got sober I wanted to believe it would last, that he had learned, that he had changed, and it would stick this time. But it never did." She met her daughter's eyes—her father's eyes. "He took you once," she said, "when he was high. You weren't even two yet and he was staying with us at the house because he was supposed to be clean. I had to go to San Francisco for a gig and the nanny didn't realize she shouldn't let him have you until you'd been gone for hours and he wasn't answering his phone. You were fine. He'd just taken you to a park, but I canceled the show and flew home and he was still high out of his mind when I got back. He didn't even have a car seat in his car for you."

She'd been so scared, flying home that night, before she knew Callie was okay. Before she knew anything. She hadn't known what to do with her daughter, but she'd always loved her, that love so big and scary that it had hurt her chest to think about it, like it was too big to fit inside her body and it was trying to burst out.

She met Callie's serious gaze. "I have a hard time forgiving him."

But she wanted Callie's forgiveness, didn't she? Was it the same thing? Did she need to let her father in? Or was she making the right call by keeping him out of Callie's life? Why didn't parenting come with a handbook? Why couldn't she look into the future and see if this time her father really would manage to stop hurting them?

"Do you miss your mom?"

Alexa's throat squeezed tight. "All the time," she murmured. "I named you after her. Did you know that? Calliope Rae." She smiled. "I thought she was the most wonderful woman in the world. She taught me to play the guitar. Did I ever tell you that?"

Callie shook her head and Alexa stood, flicking off the Christmas music and crossing to the far corner where a guitar sat propped on a stand—doubtless Victor's work, since he knew how Alexa always wanted to be able to reach for the instrument when a song crept into her brain.

She sat on the couch across from Callie, tuning the guitar and then flattening her palm against the strings. "She loved Christmas songs—especially the slow ones. *Silent Night. Away in a Manger. Oh Holy Night.* She'd play them and we'd sing and she'd always take the harmonies. Do you like to sing?"

Callie shrugged one shoulder. "I guess."

"Do you have a favorite Christmas song?" When Callie didn't answer, Alexa began plucking the strings in a familiar intro. "Do you want to hear mine?"

Her daughter met her eyes, and something incredible seemed to reach between them as she bit her lower lip, and nodded.

* * * * *

Elia woke up feeling ninety-percent human—which was pretty damn impressive considering he'd felt like three different kinds of death in the last twenty-four hours. Or what he assumed was twenty-four hours. He wasn't exactly up-to-date on the passage of time, but the clock on the bedside read five-twenty and the waning light outside the window seemed to indicate afternoon rather than morning.

He sat up in bed, waiting for the lightheadedness or the rush of a headache, but nothing happened. He felt remarkably fine. After a shower and some food, he might even work his way up to ninety-eight percent human.

His stomach growled at the thought of food—so his appetite was back, at least. He dropped his foot to the floor, listening for sounds of Alexa and Callie, wondering if they'd returned to Cold War status without him there to play mediator. He hoped not, but they were so alike—both so prickly and guarded—he wasn't ready to put money on happily-ever-after yet.

He thought he caught the slightest hint of Christmas music—they were probably watching a movie. He debated going out to greet them and let them know the twenty-four-hour bug had officially worked its way out of his system, but the pull of the shower was too strong. He could still feel the flop sweat on his skin and now that he was able to stand without swaying priority one was washing it off. Especially when he saw the rainfall showerhead.

Fifteen minutes of pure bliss later, his humanity recharged and his hair still damp from the shower, Elia pushed open the door to the master bedroom and wandered down the hall in search of his girls.

The music was clearer now, an acoustic guitar and a

pair of voices, one a husky alto and another a light, thready soprano singing *I'll Be Home for Christmas*—and as he approached the great room he realized it wasn't a recording at all.

They were singing.

He stepped quietly, not wanting to intrude, and stopped in the shadows where the hallway let out into the larger room. Even with the audible evidence that Alexa and Callie were getting into the Christmas spirit, he was still unprepared for the sight that greeted him.

The great room had been transformed. Strands of lights decorated the tree, along with far more ornaments than he remembered buying at the fair. Swags of garland draped the fireplace, where three stockings had been hung with care. It looked like a Christmas movie in here—complete with the touching mother/daughter sing-along.

Alexa cradled the guitar, playing by feel and glancing only occasionally down at her hands, her attention fixed on her daughter, who watched her just as steadily. They sang the final line of the song and the last chord faded away, the silence in the room somehow soft and welcoming.

"We should probably check on Elia," Alexa murmured, and he took that as his cue.

"Did I hear my name?" He stepped into the light of the great room and Alexa's gaze snapped to his as Callie leapt up from her chair.

"Elia!" Callie rushed to fling her arms around his waist. "You're alive."

He chuckled at her dramatics. "It's a miracle."

Alexa stood as well, her eyes searching his face. "How are you feeling?"

"Better. Must have been a twenty-four hour thing."

Her brow wrinkled in concern. "Are you sure you should be moving around?"

"We saved the star for you," Callie interrupted and he focused on the younger Miss Rae.

"Did you?"

"We couldn't reach it," Alexa admitted sheepishly.

He grinned. "Good to know I'm good for something." He made a show of looking around the room. "You two have been busy."

Callie's brow wrinkled with worry in a mirror of her mother's earlier expression. "Is it okay we started without you? We thought it would be a nice surprise—"

"It's an amazing surprise," he corrected. "The best gift I could ever ask for."

Callie bounced a little. "We have gifts too! Look!" She pointed to a small collection of presents he hadn't noticed beneath the tree.

"Where did those come from?"

"Victor," Alexa explained. "He sent the presents that would normally be at the house. They arrived this afternoon."

"Can we put the star on now?" Callie begged, hanging off his arm. "It isn't a *tree* until it has a star."

Alexa's small grin indicated she'd heard this declaration several times already, and Elia felt something stir in his chest at the new ease between them.

"It sounds like we need to put a star on," Elia said with a smile.

"Are you sure you're all right to be out of bed?" Alexa whispered—her hand on his arm making him think of an entirely different reason for being in bed, though he knew she wasn't thinking along those lines so he nipped that thought in the bud. She was his employer. His insanely hot employer, yes, but that was a line he wouldn't cross.

"I'm invincible," he insisted—and her eyes searched his, something passing between them in that look. Something that shouldn't be passing anywhere. He looked away, making his tone jocular, "Hungry, though. I could eat an entire gingerbread house. I vote after we get this star on the tree we postpone any further decorating until after dinner."

Her smile was warm and sweet and soft—and he avoided looking at it head on. "Deal."

Callie started to hand him the star, but instead of taking it, he lifted her to his shoulders and moved closer so she could place the topper on the tree herself. He lowered Callie to the floor and they all stepped back to admire the result.

"It's perfect," Callie breathed—and Elia looked down at her, something tightening in his chest at the wonder in her eyes.

"Perfect," Alexa agreed, leaning into him slightly so her shoulder brushed his arm.

"Perfect," Elia echoed, something heavy sinking into his gut.

He couldn't disagree—it felt entirely too perfect with Callie in front of him and Alexa at his side—but he didn't let himself want moments like this anymore. It was too easy for them to be taken away.

Things were getting better now. Alexa and Callie were obviously on the right track…and he needed to put some distance between him and these two before his heart was mired in the quicksand of moments like this. Don't get close. Don't get attached. He'd learned that lesson the hard way—by having his heart ripped out of his chest.

He needed to put things back on a professional level, stat. But still he couldn't make himself pull away.

Not just yet.

CHAPTER NINETEEN:
PROXIMITY WARNING

Elia was acting weird.

Alexa first noticed it as they were throwing together sandwiches for dinner. He kept sidling away from her—but not only from her, from Callie as well. Alexa rationalized that he was just trying to avoid giving them his germs—though if they hadn't already caught whatever he had, she figured the worst of the contagion had to have passed.

He was unusually quiet during dinner, letting Callie carry the conversation with descriptions of every detail of their decorative efforts, and again Alexa rationalized that he must still be tired—he was still recovering, after all.

But when they sat down for an after-dinner movie and he made a point of tinkering with the fire until both she and Callie were settled on the couch before taking the spot farthest from them, Alexa started to wonder if there was something else going on.

Tonight's movie was *The Santa Clause 2*, and Alexa found herself caught up in the film more than she'd expected—a movie all about Santa finding a wife...when Elia was constantly joking about being Santa.

Had he picked up on the crush she seemed to have developed for him? Was that why he was being so distant? He'd been all but delirious when she'd helped him to bed last night—did he remember his crack about getting her into bed? *She* certainly couldn't stop thinking about it. Was he overcompensating by keeping his distance, trying to reassure her that he wasn't going to make a pass? Or was there something else going on?

If it was just about keeping things friendly between them for Callie's sake, why was he pulling away from Callie as well?

When the credits rolled, Callie said goodnight and stood up, taking herself off to get ready for bed without being prompted. Alexa watched her go, but didn't get up to follow.

Elia stood. "I should change the sheets in the master for you."

"You should sleep in there tonight," Alexa protested. "You're still recovering."

"I'll be good on the pull-out," he insisted, already moving down the hall.

After he was gone, her gaze went to the flames in the fireplace as her thoughts churned. She'd had a great day with Callie. An amazing day. They'd made it their mission to create a magical Christmas paradise for Elia and for the first time it hadn't felt like they were both self-conscious of every action. Something was actually building there.

She'd been so excited to show Elia everything they'd done—and to share with him how it felt to have hope that she might actually be able to build a relationship with Callie. The hope that Callie might actually *want* that. And at first when he'd woken up it had been perfect. He'd smiled, he'd lifted Callie up to put the star on the tree, but then, like a switch had flipped, he'd turned off. The Smiling Samoan faded in the distance he'd put between them.

And she had no idea what she'd done wrong.

She heard his footsteps coming back down the hall, but didn't look away from the fire. "Are you okay?" she asked, only then turning to look at him.

"Of course." He sank back down on the couch, as far as he could get from her. "I looked in on Callie. She's already out."

"She had a long day and I don't think she slept much last night. She was worried about you." She lowered her voice. "We both were."

"Understandable. It'd be hard to find a replacement bodyguard to work through the holidays."

"Elia." He had to know he was more than an employee. Seeing him laid out by the flu had brought home that he'd become as necessary to her as Victor. Like family. Or something more...

She could tell herself that it was a bad idea because of Callie, but what could possibly be better for her daughter than having a man like Elia in her life? What could be better for both of them? He was extraordinary. And she was falling for him—a truth so inevitable it felt like it had always been there beneath the surface and she'd only had to open her eyes to see it shining there.

"Elia," she repeated, softer, and their eyes met, something arcing between them, a sharp, unexpected jolt of awareness.

He cleared his throat, leaning forward as if to get up. "I should—"

"Are you mad at me?" she heard herself blurt out.

He frowned, breaking eye contact. "Of course not."

"I thought you might be," she admitted, the words rushing past all her filters without her permission. "I thought maybe you were uncomfortable with how much we've been relying on you. You've been so great and I don't want you to think that I would take advantage. Or that I expect anything from you. I know you were just joking and half out of your mind when you said that thing, you know, about getting me into bed."

* * * * *

Elia froze, utterly unsure for the first time in a very long time.

How had they gotten *here*? With one of the sexiest women in the world telling him she didn't want to *take advantage* of him after he'd blurted out that he wanted her. Her vulnerability continued to shock him. It was just so damned hard to mesh the woman he saw with the one she thought she was.

"Alexa." She looked up at him then, her gaze apologetic. "I'm crazy about you." A glint of something warm lit her eyes—and he knew he needed to shut it down fast. "But this isn't a good idea. I think we both know that."

"Because of Callie?"

"Because of us. Because I don't do serious. I keep it light. I don't get attached—" *Not anymore.* "—and you deserve someone who will be all in with you."

"You don't get attached," she repeated skeptically.

"I'm Peter Pan. Ask any of my exes."

She grimaced, sinking deeper into the cushions away from him. "It's not you it's me? Is that it?"

"Sometimes it's true."

She looked away from him, into the fire. "I'm sorry if I've made you uncomfortable. I genuinely appreciate everything you've done for Callie and me."

The formality in her words stung—but he'd asked for it. He'd turned her down. This was what he wanted, right? "It's been my pleasure. She's a great kid."

"She is. And maybe with a little luck she won't turn out as messed up as her mother."

"Hey. Don't do that." He reached across the distance separating them and caught her hand. "You're amazing. You deserve someone who can give you everything."

She looked up at him, raw and unfiltered. "I think you're lying," she whispered.

"What?"

"I think you do get attached. I think you are attached and it scares you shitless. I think you're pushing me away and Callie and your sister because you're scared to feel again—it's not some noble bullshit about being for our own good, even if that's what you tell yourself. I think you don't want to want me because it makes you feel out of control—and you want control as much as I do. Because life keeps knocking you off balance and you just want to be able to stand firm for a little while. I think you're scared—and I know a lot about being scared. I have lived my life being scared—of not being good enough, of falling off the pedestal, of letting everyone down. You were the first person who made me feel like I didn't have to be scared and now what? You're just going to bail on me because it feels too real?"

"Alexa…"

"Don't do that. Don't tell me I'm amazing and you're crazy about me and I deserve the best and that's why you can't be with me. Man up. Give me the best. Be what you think I need. Because I don't think anyone else can be."

"This isn't a good idea," he said, offering the last shred of resistance he could muster—

And she closed the distance between them, throwing one leg over his lap and bracing her hands on his upper arms. "Fuck good ideas. Try the naughty list for a change," she murmured, throaty and low—and then she kissed him.

Thank God.

The rightness of it seared through him, burning away his self-preservation instincts in a volcanic rush. She was gorgeous. He knew that. Hell, all of America knew that. But all of America didn't know how she kissed. Seductive and sweet and then leaning in, making a needy noise in the back of her throat and wrapping her arms around his neck, pulling herself closer, deepening, taking everything and giving back more.

This thing between them had been building since the second he clapped eyes on her and now that he had her in his arms, the idea of letting her go was unthinkable. He wrapped his arms around her, tugging her tight against his chest, then flipped them both, pinning her to the couch cushions, reveling in the desperation of her, as if letting up for a second would make the entire illusion pop like a soap bubble. He felt the same way—like even the slightest hesitation opened a window for doubt and he couldn't allow any in—not when she tasted so nice and felt so naughty in his arms.

Alexa Rae was off-limits, out of his league—and absolutely irresistible.

God, he needed her.

He didn't know how long they kissed like that—on and on for days or weeks or years—but when she finally broke away they were both breathing heavily and her hands were fisted in his shirt. "Take this off," she demanded.

He had just enough sanity left to remember there was a nine-year-old in the house—and though Callie had been out cold, Talia had taught him that requests for midnight snacks or bedtime stories or an extra glass of water could come at any time.

"Not here," he growled, rolling her back to his lap before standing and lifting Alexa with him all in one motion. She gasped and tightened her legs around his waist—and he palmed her ass, more to angle her closer than because he was in any danger of dropping her. She was feather light, holding on tight, her breasts flattened against his chest as she kissed the side of his neck and he tried to remember the way back to the master bedroom.

The hallway. Right. End of the hall. He could do this.

As soon as he kicked the bedroom door shut behind them, her mouth was back on his. Her demand that he strip temporarily forgotten, they fell into another eternity of hungry, insatiable kisses, broken only when he lowered them onto the bed. She turned her face against the fresh, cool sheets. "Are you okay?" she gasped.

Okay? He had a fucking fireplace iron in his pants and was slowly being boiled from the inside out, but she wanted to know if he was okay? "Fine," he grunted, adjusting himself—and wondering if he would do permanent damage if he didn't get his pants off soon.

"You were so sick..." She twisted against him. "Are you sure you're up to it?"

She kept speaking, but his higher neural function had shut down when she moved against him. "Baby, believe me. I'm up." Any more up and he was going to black out from lack of blood to his brain, since it was all headed to the south pole at the moment.

She snorted—who knew the great Alexa Rae liked dirty humor—but shoved at his shoulder. "That wasn't what I meant."

"I know." He concentrated on breathing and felt

something resembling rational thought try to penetrate the haze of his brain. "I'm fine." Dying of lust, but fine. About to make the biggest mistake of his life, but fine. "But this is a bad idea—"

"No." Her arms and legs tightened around him and he groaned at the sudden pressure of her pelvis against his fly. She released a breathy little pant. "Please?"

Oh fuck. He was a goner. He was a fucking goner. Stupid. So stupid. But that little panted plea reached inside him and yanked and there was no physical way he could walk away now. Especially when she was kissing him.

He groaned into her mouth.

Peter Pan didn't do real. Peter Pan didn't do vulnerable. But the shell of the irresponsible boy he'd been playing at being since he lost Talia cracked and something real reached in and grabbed his chest, right where his heart should be. This woman, this rock star, got to him. He could fight it all he wanted, but there was no going back now.

"Oh God, baby, you make me crazy," he whispered against her skin. "You feel so good."

You, you, always you. He banned himself from saying I. Because he knew what would happen when he did. The words that would follow. And he couldn't let himself tell Alexa Rae that he loved her. Even if it might be true.

CHAPTER TWENTY:
EVERYTHING FALLS…

"Mom! Elia, wake up! It snowed!"

Alexa jerked awake, flinging her arm to the side in an instinctive attempt to shove Elia over the side of the bed so Callie wouldn't see him if she burst into the room— only to find there was nothing beside her but pillows. She wound up flailing, tangled in the covers before she could get her arms free.

"Elia?" she hissed out a whisper, using the Force and every other nonexistent brand of telepathy she could to try to keep Callie outside the room. Was he in the bathroom?

She wasn't ashamed of what had happened—but they hadn't exactly defined what they were last night and Callie was already so attached to him that it wouldn't take much to tip her over into seeing them as one big, happy family. It was too much. Too complicated.

Even if he had said he loved her last night.

That was in the heat of the moment. In the light of day, she was panicking just thinking about her daughter finding him in here with her—

Until she realized the bathroom door was open and the sound she was hearing was not him brushing his teeth, but someone moving around in the kitchen at the front of the house.

He'd already left. Of course he had. She wasn't disappointed about that. This wasn't disappointment she was feeling, this heavy, nervous feeling that last night had only been a one night stand and didn't mean anything. She'd *wanted* him to sneak out before Callie saw him, but somehow the fact that he had made her feel...unsettled.

"Mo-om! Come *on!*"

Alexa cursed softly under her breath and scrambled out of bed, pulling on a pair of yoga pants and a soft t-shirt. She tugged her hair into a ponytail to try to hide the why-yes-someone-*did*-run-his-hands-through-it-last-night look and padded barefoot down the hallway to where Callie bounded around the great room.

"Look! It snowed! Real snow!" She raced over, grabbing Alexa's hand and dragging her to the largest of the windows so they could admire the pristine white covering everything. From Callie's excitement, she'd half expected Snowpocalypse levels of pile-up, but what greeted her instead was two lovely inches dusting the deck and clinging to the trees.

"Wow. I guess Santa was listening."

Callie rolled her eyes—far too jaded to credit Santa— but her smile didn't wane. "Can I go play in it?"

"Breakfast is in fifteen minutes," Elia called out from the kitchen, proving he'd been listening in.

Alexa didn't turn to face him—not quite ready for that yet—nodding to Callie. "Just for ten minutes. We'll go out again after breakfast."

Callie squealed and raced off to pile on her outer layers, already fully dressed. What time was it? Alexa didn't think she'd slept in that long, but Callie looked like she'd been awake for hours. Or maybe the sight of snow had kicked her into warp speed.

With Callie launching herself out the front door with a whoop, Alexa turned to face the man in the kitchen. He gave her a distracted smile as she approached, most of his attention on the bacon he was turning.

"We got our snow," she commented, awkwardness crawling up her spine.

"It's a Christmas miracle." He flashed her a quick grin.

"God bless us every one?" she said, trying for a joking tone.

"Are you implying I'm tiny?"

"I wouldn't dare," she swore—but the banter felt tentative. A little forced.

He wasn't looking at her—which, yes was a good thing when he was cooking and they didn't want to be consumed in a grease fire, but she needed him to reassure her that he didn't regret what they'd done last night. She needed him to look at her in a way that made her believe he really meant what he'd whispered into her hair that last time. Those three little words. She hadn't said them back and now she couldn't help wondering if he was regretting them. The harsh light of day was a little too harsh for her taste—even if it was beautiful and snowy.

She started to move past him, needing to do something, even if it was only setting the table, when he suddenly turned off the heat on the stove and reached for her. His palm flat on her stomach stopped her in her tracks. "Alexa. About last night—"

Victor's ringtone sang through the room, interrupting whatever Elia would have said. Alexa hadn't even remembered leaving her phone in here last night after dinner, but she must have. It sat on the counter, blaring cheerfully.

"I'll call him back," she said, needing to hear whatever Elia had been about to say, but he was already turning back to the stove.

"No, take it. Breakfast is almost ready."

Crap.

Frustrated, she snatched up her phone, accepting the call right as it was about to go to voicemail. "Victor. Merry Christmas." It was still the day before Christmas Eve, but even she could get into the spirit.

"Alexa." An ominous pause. "You haven't seen yet."

Shit. She didn't need any more words. His tone alone told her everything she needed to know. Victor was in damage control mode. Some shit somewhere in her career had just hit a fan. All that remained now was to learn which one and how badly. "What happened?"

Elia looked up from the stove, his attention caught by the suddenly serious tone of her voice, but she waved him off. Whatever it was, it wouldn't be tragic—just potentially career ending. She racked her brain trying to figure out what it could be, but she couldn't think of anything scandal worthy that had happened in her life lately. Not that the tabloids needed real scandals. They were perfectly willing to make them up. All it took was one person willing to go on record with tall tales. And there were plenty of those in showbiz. All looking to springboard themselves to fame.

"There's an article—that asshole Torrence. He's going to get sued one of these days. The other sites are just quoting it and using a lot of allegedlies to cover their asses, but it's everywhere now." Victor paused heavily. "Alexa, it's about Callie."

The words reverberated through her, gong like, but Victor was still speaking.

"About you and Callie, specifically. It calls you an unfit mother. Says you don't even know how old she is—"

Alexa's head jerked toward where Elia was scooping eggs onto plates, an invisible fist slamming into her chest. *You don't even know how old she is.* "Who?" she interrupted Victor. "Who's the source?"

A tiny, hesitant pause. "We aren't sure yet. Torrence didn't reveal the name, but at one point he did indicate his source was male. He could have been lying to confuse things—"

But Alexa couldn't hear anymore.

She'd slept with him. He'd sold her out to the tabloids—and he hadn't even had to lie. It was all true. She was a horrible mother. Yes, he'd signed a non-disclosure agreement and she could sue his ass, but he'd probably gotten a big enough payday to make it worth his while.

And she'd slept with him.

"Honey, your fans are seeing this. We need to react-"

But Elia looked up from his culinary efforts then, concern flashing across his face when he saw her expression, and Alexa couldn't deal with Victor or her fans or the tour ticket sales right now. She could only handle one thing at a time and that thing was the large man in her kitchen whom she'd never really known.

God, she was an idiot.

"I'll call you back, Victor." She thumbed off the call while he was still speaking.

"Is everything okay?" Elia asked—as if he didn't know. Playing innocent. He was a much better actor than she'd given him credit for. She should have known. In LA, everyone was an actor-slash-something. Actor-bodyguard wouldn't be anything new.

"Did you sell me out to the tabloids?" Her voice sounded remarkably calm. Almost emotionless.

Elia frowned. "What?"

"There's a story about Callie and me. About how I'm a terrible mother and don't even know her age. Did you talk to the press?"

Something flashed across his face before his expression tightened down hard. "Don't be ridiculous."

"You can tell me." Her voice still sounded so incredibly calm—the Oscar voters should be watching now. This was award caliber stuff. "Was it when I fired you? I would understand. Maybe you were mad, wanted to get back at me—"

His expression darkened. "This is crazy."

The front door burst open, Callie tripping inside, lightly coated in snow. "Is breakfast ready?"

"Go to your room, Callie," Alexa demanded without taking her eyes off Elia. It was instinctive. Automatic. The need to get her baby *away from him*.

"Mom?"

"*Now*, Callie!"

She heard the thud of feet as her daughter bolted down the hall. Elia frowned after her. "You didn't have to scare her—"

"I don't even know her age? Sound familiar?"

"You got her age wrong on national television! Anyone with Google could be the source."

Her chest felt tight—she was pretty sure she wasn't having a heart attack, but it was hard to tell. "You still haven't denied it."

"Are you serious?" he snapped. "No, I didn't talk to the press. Or anyone else. Happy?"

She stared at him, trying to see through him, trying to see the truth, but she just wasn't sure if she could trust him. She'd let her feelings blind her, but how well did she really know him?

Her father, Dare, now Elia... all the men in her life let her down. Except Victor—but Victor was paid to look after her. Paid to keep her working. Paid to keep her succeeding. Who could she really trust just because they cared? No one. She should have learned that lesson long ago, but she kept making the same damn mistakes. Following her stupid heart down the wrong path. Falling in love with the wrong man...

She couldn't deal with that. Not right now. So she focused on something she could. "I need to go back to LA."

She hadn't been able to identify Elia's expression, but now it was clear. Disappointment. "Why, Alexa? What's running back to LA going to fix? Stay here. Be with Callie. Show her that she matters more than some story—"

"You don't understand. We have to do damage control. My fans are seeing this. Callie and I need to go back to LA—"

"And what? Be seen holding hands and getting ice cream like the perfect mommy-daughter couple? You think the tabloids won't see right through that since you've never done it before in the past? Maybe instead of pretending to be a good mom, you could stay here and be one." She flinched and regret flashed across his face. "I'm sorry—"

"I think you should go," she interrupted. "You can take the SUV. Victor will arrange to have a car come pick us up."

"Alexa, come on. Don't do this."

She'd trusted him. How could she have trusted him? "You need to go."

"Seriously? That's it? After everything?" He shook his head—his face vivid with disgust, frustration, and something else she wasn't prepared to identify.

"I can't think with you here," she snapped.

He dropped the spatula. "Fine."

He stalked out of the kitchen and she heard him in the loft, gathering up his things, but she couldn't seem to move, temporarily paralyzed. Part of her was terrified of having to look at him again while another part fervently prayed he would come back into the kitchen and somehow erase everything that had happened in the last fifteen minutes.

She wanted to be back in their awkward morning after, not in this awful, constricting place where she felt like she was suffocating just listening to him clomp down the loft stairs. She held her breath—would he come in here? Tell her she was wrong? That he did love her like he'd whispered last night, so softly she'd almost thought she imagined the words?

But he didn't. The front door opened and closed. Booted footsteps retreated.

Leaving Alexa alone with three plates of cooling eggs and a daughter she prayed would understand.

CHAPTER TWENTY-ONE:
APART

"Mom?"

As if conjured by the thought of her, Callie appeared at the edge of the kitchen—and Alexa's paralysis lifted. "I'm sorry, baby," she murmured. "Sorry I yelled at you."

Callie frowned. "Where's Elia going?"

Alexa's breath hitched and she reached for the lukewarm eggs. "Come have breakfast. There's something I need to talk to you about."

Callie trailed her to the table, her eyes wide and nervous. Remembering how her daughter had reacted the last time Alexa had thrown Elia out, her stomach clenched and she poked at her eggs with her fork rather than trying to eat, trying to find a place to start.

"You know with my job there will always be people who want to use us. I've always tried to protect you from that as much as I could, and sometimes I ended up keeping you at a distance when I shouldn't have." She swallowed, forcing herself to look up from the eggs. "I've made a lot of mistakes where you're concerned. I should have been around more. But I want to be better. I want to be everything you need. I want you to always know that I will be there for you and to never doubt for a second how much I love you." She met her daughter's somber gaze and swallowed down the emotion choking off her words. "I love you like crazy, kiddo. And from here on out, whatever we do, we do it together, okay? You and me."

Callie nodded, her eyes wide and serious.

Alexa took a breath, trying to find the right words. "Someone told some reporters some things about us. About our private lives. Someone close to us. I don't know for sure who it was and I really hope it wasn't Elia—" Her voice broke on his name and she swallowed again. "But until we know for sure, I asked him to go. I have to protect you." She reached out, brushing the hair behind Callie's ear. "I'm going to have Uncle Victor send someone to pick us up and we'll go home tonight."

Her daughter's lip didn't even tremble and Alexa couldn't help wondering if Callie was experiencing the same strange out-of-body paralysis she'd felt at the idea of Elia's betrayal of their trust. "Do we have to go back to LA? I like it here."

"I like it too," Alexa murmured. "But it's time to go home."

She looked around the rental, feeling sick and stupid for how completely she'd bought into the fantasy they'd woven here. Into the big happy family and the idea that he could really love her.

Just another man who would let her down.

"We'll get a great tree in LA," Alexa promised.

Callie nodded, eating quietly.

"I'm sorry, baby," Alexa said softly when Callie set down her fork. "I'm so sorry I'm not better."

Callie shrugged and slid her chair back. Alexa thought she would go, but she moved to Alexa's side and climbed into her lap. Her daughter hugged her and Alexa squeezed her eyes shut. "It's okay, Mom," Callie said. "You're mine."

* * * * *

Elia spent the first twenty minutes of the drive righteously pissed. Pissed at Alexa for not letting him even say goodbye to Callie—again—though he'd been so angry when he'd walked out that he hadn't been in any state to talk to her. Pissed at Alexa for suspecting him. Pissed at himself for letting himself get that close.

Then he'd stopped for gas, pulled out his phone to see exactly what she was accusing him of and he'd gotten angry for a whole new reason.

The first few articles he found were vague, referring to allegations from a "source close to the family," but after a few clicks he found the one that had apparently started it all and he began to feel sick. It was carefully worded—implying that Alexa was borderline abusive without ever actually accusing her.

But the comments. The comments didn't imply anything. They accused. They shamed. They raged.

People were calling for a boycott of her film and her tour. Some had already started burning her albums on social media. Campaigns had been started to call child services repeatedly until *something was done*. These people, who had never met Alexa or Callie, were convinced they knew the truth, and all too eager to judge and condemn.

Elia knew Alexa would never allow any harm to come to Callie. The girl was loved. She was cared for. And now people who had never met either of them were calling for Callie to be taken away from her mother—right when they'd found one another. Because of an article.

And because, as one commenter so eloquently put it,

there's nothing so satisfying as watching the mighty bitches fall.

Elia pointed the car back toward Tahoe. She might be pissed at him, but it was still his job to protect her. He hooked up his Bluetooth and called Candy as he drove.

"Have you seen this?" he asked, after they dispensed with the usual greetings.

"Total shitstorm," Candy said, not unsympathetic.

"Can you find out who the source is?"

"Already on it. There's always a digital trail."

"Let me know when you find it, okay?"

"Roger."

His next call was to Victor. He wasn't entirely sure the manager would answer, so as soon as he did Elia wasted no time making his case.

"I had nothing to do with it."

"I don't know whether you did or not," Victor said after a measured pause. "I just know Alexa was awfully upset when she thought you had. You wanna tell me why she was so upset?"

Elia felt like a teenager who'd just been caught making out with his girlfriend by her father. "I took a drive to give her some space," he said, creatively massaging the truth, "but I'm on my way back to the house now. Do you think you can convince her not to start throwing knives the second I walk through the door?"

"She isn't there."

Elia tightened his grip on the steering wheel. "You got a driver out there that fast?"

"She took a taxi to the airfield. We chartered a flight. Should be taking off any minute."

Elia cursed under his breath, pulling off at the next turn out and pointing the car south again. So much for charging to the rescue. "Is there anything I can do? I'm still her bodyguard."

"That's what you're calling it?" Victor asked, and Elia found himself fighting another blush.

"I want to help," he insisted.

"Right now the best thing you can do is go home. And let me know if you find out who went after our girls."

It dug under his skin, not being with her. With them. He should have fought. He should have stayed. But he'd been scared shitless when he woke up beside her this morning, scared by all that he'd said, and as soon as she'd accused him he'd leapt at the chance to run. But now... now he had to do whatever he could to get back.

"Will do," he promised, setting a course for LA.

* * * * *

The paparazzi were lined up three deep outside the gates. Alexa hunkered down, hiding behind giant Breakfast at Tiffany's style sunglasses and tucking Callie under her coat to shield her from view as high-powered flashes tried to penetrate the tinted windows of the car.

"You'd think they'd have somewhere better to be two days before Christmas," she muttered as the gates closed behind them, locking out the worst of the storm.

For now.

She'd learned long ago never to read what people wrote about her online, but she'd had to know what they were saying about Callie so while on the flight she'd caved and looked. It wasn't pretty. The original article was more innuendo than anything else, but the exaggeration train had taken off and was only gathering speed.

Would Callie be embarrassed to go back to school

after Christmas break? Would her tour be canceled?

Would someone try to take Callie away?

That last thought so horrified her that her brain couldn't seem to get past it. Every time she thought it, her mind shuddered to a stop and she had to fight to keep it together.

Yes, she had trouble getting close to people—even her own daughter—but she'd always tried to give Callie the best in life. Always. And now they'd finally figured out how to be together, how to be family, and this had to happen.

"Can we go pick out a new tree?" Callie asked as the car stopped and Victor rushed out of the house to greet them.

"We can't go out, baby, but we'll get one brought in right away, okay? A really big one. Do you think it would look good in the living room?"

Callie shrugged. She'd been quiet ever since Tahoe.

Victor met them, giving Alexa a quick hug and patting Callie's shoulder. "Come on. Let's get inside. No telling how many vultures in helicopters are circling."

Alexa cringed and looked up—but didn't see any photographers dangling from helicopters. Maybe they'd decided to take the day off to do good deeds. It was Christmas after all. She could only hope.

"We need a tree, Victor," she said, in what she hoped was an authentically cheerful tone. "A big one. Do you think we can have one delivered this afternoon?"

"Absolutely." He matched her tone. "Do you think you and Mia can get out the Christmas decorations while I talk to your mom, Callie?"

Callie nodded and went with Victor's assistant, though she glanced back over her shoulder, visibly reluctant to leave Alexa. She would have liked the thought that Callie wanted to stay with her, if not for the reason behind it. Her daughter couldn't miss that something was very wrong today, no matter how Alexa tried to shield her from it.

"Victor," Alexa said, her voice wobbling, as soon as Callie was out of earshot.

He hugged her again. "It's just a story. A rumor."

"Could they really take her?"

"We won't let that happen. And I doubt they'll even try. It's gossip."

"Do we know who…?"

"I have some people looking into it and Elia's got the Elite Protection people on it too." When she stiffened at his name, Victor squeezed her shoulder. "For what it's worth, I don't think it was him."

"I don't know what to think," she whispered. "I don't want it to be him, but I'm afraid the fact that I want that so badly is making it impossible for me to see the truth."

"So I take it something happened in Tahoe."

"You mean other than me completely falling for him?"

He grinned. "At least you have good taste."

"Are you sure? Are we sure this isn't him?" She couldn't keep the hope out of her voice.

"Honestly? No. But it isn't the kind of story I see anyone sitting on for several days and if he had leaked it when you fired him the first time, why didn't it come out until now? Seems more like some disgruntled former employee fell on hard times and thought they could get some quick cash and dodge getting sued for violating the NDA by keeping it anonymous."

"But why bring Callie into it?"

"Because she's the one thing you've never been able to handle. Until now. Is that something else I have to thank Mr. Aiavao for?"

Alexa closed her eyes, the weight of everything that had happened this morning landing on her. "I was horrible to him. He probably never wants to see me again."

"You might be surprised. Now. Let's talk business so we can get it over with and focus on important things like ordering a Christmas tree. What are our priorities?"

"Protecting Callie. Keeping her as far away from all this as possible."

He nodded. "Always. But that doesn't mean we can't fight back."

CHAPTER TWENTY-TWO:
UNEXPECTED VISITORS

Elia raised his hand to knock, hating the feeling of uncertainty that seemed to drape over him. He wasn't sure how she would react to him showing up here Christmas Eve, but he'd had to come.

He had the chance to wonder, in the time after he knocked, if she was even here. He hadn't called ahead. But then the door opened and something lifted in his chest and he knew he'd been right to come.

"*Elia.* You're here."

He smiled. "Merry Christmas, Sefina."

"Merry Christmas." His sister pulled him into a hug, smiling through unshed tears. "I thought you had to work. You said—"

"The job finished early," he explained, in a half truth. "Is the offer still open?"

"Of course, you big idiot." She swiped at her eyes and linked her arm through his, ushering him inside. "Michael's trying to figure out where he put the wine we got for tonight and Mom's in the kitchen cooking enough for twenty people. She'll be so excited to see you. *Mom!*" Sefina dragged him toward the kitchen, yelling to their mother, and Elia found himself instantly drawn into the heart of the family gathering—his mother squealed and hugged him before smacking him on the shoulder and scolding him for pretending he wasn't going to come, Michael grinned and clasped him on the arm, jokingly pleading his gratitude for providing reinforcements against the combined cheer assault that was Sefina and his mother, and Sefina watched it all with a small smile.

He'd braced for awkwardness, a layer of distance, to feel like he shouldn't be here because he wouldn't be able to fake Christmas cheer, but it didn't feel fake—and his sister knew him too well to let him get in his head. Whenever he started thinking of Talia, she would squeeze his hand and her smile would turn a little sad— and he began to realize how stupid he'd been to push away the one person who had always known exactly how he felt.

He'd needed this, he realized. He'd been so scared it would hurt—that all he would be able to think about was Talia and the fact that she wasn't there—that he'd ignored all the things that *were* still there.

The love was still there. Even if the little girl who had seemed to shine like the sun at the center of his world, shining love on everything and everyone she touched, was gone. There was still love. And the memory of Talia didn't hurt quite so much when he was surrounded by it.

Hours later, after his mother had gone to bed and Michael had excused himself to call his parents in Portland, Elia sat with Sefina at the kitchen table, tracing the stains Talia had left there. The little lingering traces of a life too short.

Sefina caught his eye, seeming to read his thoughts as her smile shifted with the memory. "I've missed you, big brother," she murmured.

For years she'd been his best friend. He'd given her

away at her wedding. Held her hand when Talia was born. Leaned on her after his accident and propped her up as best he could through the months of Talia's diagnosis and treatment, and now he felt he barely knew her. And whose fault was that? "I've missed you too." He reached for her hand, linking their fingers on the scarred wood. "I'm sorry I've been…distant."

"I understood. Even when I worried about you."

"You shouldn't have been worrying about me. You'd just lost a kid. You didn't need to be worrying about my grief—"

"So you pushed me away and tried to fix everything on your own, I know." She smiled, wryly. "I do know you, you know."

"I should have been there for you—"

"Elia." The low, firm sound of his name on her lips called up a dozen memories. She'd always been the strong one. Strong in ways no one could see. "Stop it. You're the best brother I could ever ask for, but you don't have to be perfect all the time—you know that right? You're allowed to completely fall apart sometimes too. I just wish you'd lean on me when you did. God knows I've leaned on you more times than I can count."

He grimaced. "I thought your Christmas would be better without me."

"Well, you never were the smart one," she said dryly and he snorted. "I'm glad you're back."

He swallowed around a thickness in his throat. "Me too."

He'd thought he was doing the right thing, protecting her from his grief and the reminder of hers, when really all he'd been doing was pushing her away when she needed him too. Pushing her away because he didn't think he could be the strong one for her. It had killed him that he couldn't save Talia, in the end. Killed him that there was nothing he could do. And he'd been so locked inside his own shit that he hadn't seen that Sefina was feeling the exact same way—and that pushing her away wasn't helping either of them. He'd retreated into self-preservation mode, cutting everyone off…until Callie.

And Alexa.

It had taken Alexa calling him on it to realize he was scared to feel again, scared to get attached. But if you cut yourself off from the prospect of pain, you cut yourself off from all the good stuff as well.

He'd thought he was being noble. Strong. Keeping his shit from spilling over onto anyone else. But it was all just fear.

"Are you okay?" Sefina asked gently.

"I'm good." He cleared his throat roughly—and Sefina called him on the lie with a look, as only the person who knew him best in the world could.

"I had a job that ended badly," he admitted, knowing she wouldn't press for details since he'd told her about the myriad nondisclosure agreements he always had to sign when he worked with celebrities.

"Really?" she cocked her head to the side with a small smile. "I thought it might be about a woman."

"Why does it always have to be a woman?"

"No reason," Sefina said innocently, sliding her phone across to him.

On the screen was a photo of him with Callie and Alexa. It must have been snapped while they were watching the choir at the Christmas fair. Callie was up on his shoulders, Alexa leaning against his arm, and he was looking at her like she glowed with an angelic light.

Apparently someone had snuck a cell phone picture

of them after all.

Elia flicked a finger over the screen, scanning the attached article. Alexa had evidently begun to fight back. The picture was part of a rebuttal to the original accusations—framed as a private family getaway, complete with quotes by the locals who had seen them there.

Candy had traced the source of the original article and Elia had called Victor with the information as soon as he heard, but he hadn't heard a word from Alexa's camp since then. She *knew* it wasn't him and she still hadn't called. What was he supposed to do with that?

"You looked pretty happy," Sefina commented gently.

Elia shoved away the phone. "She doesn't trust me." Even after he'd been cleared, she *still* wouldn't let him in.

"So you just give up? When did you become such a quitter?"

"Hey. I'm giving her space." He wasn't. He was flailing. He wanted her back but he didn't have the first idea how to go about it, how to make her see that his love was something she could count on.

"If you say so," Sefina muttered. "I'd just hate to think my brother was running scared."

"I'm strategizing," he insisted as the doorbell rang and Sefina turned toward the sound with a frown.

"Who—?" She stood, glancing at the clock which read nine-forty-five, and headed for the front door. "Are you expecting someone?"

* * * * *

Alexa stood on the cute little front porch, feeling unbelievably exposed. Which might have had something to do with the fact that she hadn't been alone in public in Los Angeles in nearly a decade, but probably had more to do with the reason she was here. And the man she hoped was inside.

She'd already tried his apartment. When she'd struck out there, she'd asked Victor if he'd ever given them his sister's address. Where else would he be on Christmas Eve, right?

Just in case the door bell was broken, she knocked on the brightly painted front door of the cute little bungalow and plucked at her sleeve nervously. The house couldn't be more than a thousand square feet, but it glowed with warmth and personality. And when the door popped open suddenly, so did its owner.

Elia's sister had the same beautiful dark curls from the pictures. Dark brown eyes that matched her brother's widened in shock and a startled smile curved her lips. "Holy crap, Alexa Rae."

Alexa smiled past the knot of fear clogging up her throat. "You must be Sefina. Is Elia here by any chance?"

"You know I was hoping you'd come, but I didn't think you'd actually appear at my door in the middle of the night."

"I'm sorry to come by so late," Alexa hurried to apologize. Victor had told her that Elia's people had tracked down the source of the article, but she'd wanted to wait until Callie was asleep to confront the problem. She hadn't wanted to disrupt their Christmas Eve together.

As soon as Callie had finally settled down, with Victor staying with her in case she woke up, Alexa had planned to go straight to the source...but she'd found herself driving to Elia's place instead, and then his sister's, searching for him.

"No, no, this is perfect. My idiot brother is in the kitchen." Sefina stepped back, waving her into the house and Alexa's relief and fear spiked in equal parts.

He was here. That was good, right? Good and terrifying.

He might not want to see her. She'd screwed up. She hadn't trusted him. He hadn't wanted serious and she'd practically badgered him into sleeping with her and then immediately turned around and thrown him out.

She stepped into the living room, glancing around nervously. The house was small, but warm. Sefina was obviously a woman who loved bright colors and bold statements, but somehow the mishmash of loud prints worked together in a cozy, eclectic way. It made Alexa realize how sterile her own flawlessly designed Mulholland home felt.

Until she saw Elia standing at the edge of the hallway and she forgot everything but him.

"Hi," she whispered, breathlessly. Like a bad Marilyn Monroe impersonator. *Get it together, Alexa.*

"Hi."

Then nothing. She needed him to say something, anything, but he was just watching her, his expression guarded, as if trying to deduce why she was here.

Sefina glanced back and forth between them. "I'll just go check on the, um…" She slipped past Elia into the hallway to give them privacy—shoving her brother deeper into the room with a not-so-subtle nudge as she whispered something that Alexa couldn't hear.

"I'm sorry to drop in on you like this," she said, trying to find the words she'd rehearsed on the way over here. He wasn't smiling. Elia was always smiling. A nervous laugh escaped. "I seem to be making a habit of throwing you out and then begging for forgiveness."

"Are you here because Victor told you it wasn't me?" he asked finally. "Because you had proof?"

"No. Well. Yes. Sort of. I—" God, why were words so hard?

"Why are you here, Alexa?"

"I was wondering if you could come with me," she blurted—though that wasn't at all what she'd meant to say. "To see my father. To confront him about selling us out." Elia blinked slowly, something softening slightly in his posture, and she rushed on. "I knew it wasn't you," she said earnestly. "In my heart. But I didn't know if I could trust my heart because I wanted so badly for it not to be you. You know? I should have trusted you, but I assumed the worst because I was afraid I was wrong again. I don't exactly have the best track record."

"I know," he murmured, and a little flicker of hope kindled.

"I know I don't have any right to ask, but do you think you could come with me?" She wanted more than that. She wanted him back in her life all the way. She wanted to tell him she was crazy in love with him. But when he wasn't smiling it was so damn scary to say.

She held her breath, hoping his serious frown would crack, but he didn't smile as he nodded. "Of course."

* * * * *

He didn't know what he was doing.

Elia sat in the driver's seat of one of Alexa's SUVs, resisting the urge to drum his fingers on the steering wheel as they both stared at the rundown apartment building where her father was apparently living.

He'd wanted a way back into Alexa's good graces. He'd been hoping for this. So why hadn't he swept her into his arms the second he saw her in Sefina's living room?

When he'd seen her, all he'd been able to think was that she would never trust him all the way—and he understood why. Her own father had sold a story about how she was a horrible mother, and the father of her child hadn't exactly been a paragon of trustworthiness either. But how could they build a relationship without trust? Would she always suspect him first when anything went wrong?

Or were all of those doubts, which had sprung up the second he saw her standing nervously in Sefina's living room, just another way of keeping distance between them and protecting himself?

He should tell her he loved her. Take the leap. But instead he sat beside her and frowned at the building.

"Maybe he isn't home," Alexa whispered. It had begun to drizzle, a slight, miserable rain, as if even in LA the weather knew this occasion called for it.

"You don't have to talk to him. Not tonight," Elia reminded her, but she shook her head.

"Yes, I do."

"Do you want me to come in with you?"

"Yes?" she said uncertainly. "But I should probably do this alone."

"I'm right here," he reminded her, infusing the words with all that still remained unsaid between them. He would always be right here. Always.

Alexa caught his eye, smiling slightly though it never reached her eyes, and moved quickly, as if trying to be out of the car and up the stairs to the second floor exterior hallway before she could lose her momentum.

CHAPTER TWENTY-THREE:
UNFINISHED BUSINESS

It had been five years since she'd seen her father in person.

At the time, he'd been in rehab—again. Going through the steps toward sobriety—again. And he'd wanted to apologize—again. But his attempt at amends had ended the way all of his previous attempts had—with excuses. And with a request for money.

Ever since she'd cut him off financially, that was how it went.

He could say he loved her, but he couldn't ever seem to show it. He could promise to do better, but he could never keep those promises.

She used to wonder if things would have been different if her mother hadn't died in the accident. He hadn't been drinking then—at least he said he hadn't—but he'd still blamed himself for the crash. He'd been driving and he'd survived, so he'd spent the rest of his life hating himself for it. She knew all that. She just didn't know if it would have been different if the roads hadn't been so slick that night.

If her mother had lived, would she have grown up with the perfect nuclear family? Did such a thing really exist? Who would she be in that alternate universe? Would she still be a singer if she hadn't felt driven to music to try to cling to the memory of her mother? Would she be a star if she weren't trying to fill a hole left by loss with fame? Would she be happy? Would she know how to trust?

But wondering all that didn't help anything. And she couldn't wish for that alternate universe. Not now. Not when it might mean she never had Callie. The past didn't matter anymore. Only the future mattered. And Elia had shown her that her future didn't have to be defined by what had come before.

Alexa dropped her fist on the door.

She heard the shuffling inside, the familiar grumbling before the door opened two inches, the chain holding it in place. Her father's eyes—exactly like her own, and Callie's—stared out at her for a single silent moment before he shut the door and reopened it, swinging it open without the chain. "The prodigal daughter returns."

He'd been drinking. She recognized it instantly and the confirmation that he hadn't changed made something inside her simultaneously sink and settle with a strange sort of peace.

"Won't you come in?" he asked, mockingly waving a hand inside.

"I'm good right here." Standing under the overhang with the sound of the rain dripping behind her.

He didn't look bad. His hair was a little long and his shirt was untucked, but she'd seen him in much worse condition.

"I was sober until two days ago," he informed her, as if she should be proud of him.

"Is that when you got the money for the article?"

His eyes narrowed. "I didn't say anything lots of other people don't already know."

"Yeah, but you said it to the press. You sold out your own family."

"My family ignores me," he snapped. "My precious daughter won't talk to me or let me see my grandchild."

"You didn't want to see me. You wanted money. You think I don't know that by now?"

"It's not like you don't have enough to spare. I raised you. Don't I deserve—"

"I don't think you want to get into a conversation about what you deserve. Or how great a job you did raising me."

"I tried," he whined, that plaintive, helpless note entering his voice.

"I know. And it was never your fault you didn't succeed," she snapped. "Not at getting clean. Not at taking care of me when I needed you. You always had an excuse, but I'm not here to listen to excuses. I'm here because…because…" For a moment she flailed, suddenly unsure why she'd come at all. What was she doing here? It was Christmas Eve. This was when all the Christmas movies said you should be with family. This was when miracles happened, but he wasn't her miracle. Callie was. Elia was.

The truth slid through her, simple and right. "I'm here because I need to forgive you," she murmured, rain pattering softly behind her. "I need to do that for myself. But that doesn't mean I have to let you back into my life. You have to earn that, Dad, and selling me out to the tabloids isn't a good way to start." She swallowed thickly. "I don't know if I'm ever going to trust you again, but you're still my dad and I love you even when I hate you. So if you want to get sober, for real, I'll help with that as much as I can, but I have to look out for me and Callie and what we need. And until you change that can't be you. You can sell as many stories as you want, or you can step up and be the man you could have been if we'd never lost her. Be the guy she'd want you to be, Dad. Please. For both of us."

He swayed, but he didn't say a word—and she could only hope he was sober enough to understand.

She didn't know what else to say. *Merry Christmas* and *goodbye* both felt equally wrong, so she nodded farewell and stepped back into the rain without another word. He didn't call after her. He didn't speak at all, watching her go without closing the door.

It wasn't raining hard, but icy droplets slid down the back of her neck as she made her way down the exterior stairs. She looked up as she descended and there he was. Elia. Standing beside the car in the rain. Watching her. Watching over her.

Alexa's throat tightened at the sight of him and she went straight into his arms, wrapping her own around his waist and burying her face against his chest as his strength closed around her.

"You all right?" he rumbled, and she nodded against his chest, keeping her eyes squeezed shut tight. Just holding on.

Safe. Home.

"I'm sorry," she whispered, tipping her face up so she could see the tiny droplets of rain clinging to his dark lashes. "I should have trusted you. It was me I didn't trust. I've never been good at knowing who to love."

His eyebrows arched up, a small smile quirking his lips. "Love, huh?"

"I know it's crazy. We just met and I barely know you...but I know you, Elia. And you're the best man I've ever known, the best thing that's ever happened to me and I felt like someone carved my heart out of my chest when I thought I was wrong about you. I felt so stupid for loving you. So stupid for wanting more. And I *hated* the idea that you could have betrayed me, but I've been wrong before. It seems like I'm always wrong when I fall for someone, so how do you trust when something is suddenly right? When it seems too good to be true?"

"Alexa—"

She'd wanted so badly for him to speak, but now she couldn't let him. She was too scared of what he would say. "You probably think I'm mistaking gratitude or great sex for love, but I'm not. Callie and I are good now. That isn't why I need you. I love you. *We* love you. And I don't expect you to feel the same way. I know I'm high maintenance and a total mess and you have your family—And I know you aren't serious, that you didn't want serious. I get that—"

"*Alexa.* Stop."

Her mouth snapped shut with an audible click.

He gave her a little shake, a smile curving his lips. "Don't let the smile fool you. I'm a very serious man. And I'm very serious about you. I love you so much it scares the shit out of me."

"It does?" Her voice warbled hopefully.

He cupped her face in his hands, lowering his head so their foreheads almost touched. "Losing Talia was the worst thing I ever felt. I didn't want to feel anything like that ever again. I told myself if I never let anyone close again, I'd be safe—but I couldn't just choose not to love you. I couldn't help it. You and Callie. You Rae women snuck into my heart when I wasn't looking and took over. And when you threw me out—"

"I'm sorry! I'm so sorry about that—I freaked out—"

"Baby, I know. And all I could think about was

getting you back." His grin tipped up higher on one side. "And making sure you knew that you can always trust me. That I will *always* be there for you."

He would. She knew it. She went up on her tiptoes, gripping his lapels to hold him close. "I'll always be there for you too. I promise."

He smiled. "I'm gonna hold you to that."

He kissed her then, holding her close, so soft and sweet and perfect that for the first time in her jaded life, Alexa Rae believed in miracles.

And when she opened her eyes, it had started to snow, right there in Los Angeles.

EPILOGUE:
MIRACLES EVERYWHERE

"Are you sure you aren't Santa Claus?"

Alexa leaned against Elia on Christmas morning watching it snow. In LA.

Admittedly they were inside a soundstage on one of the studio lots and the snow was all fake, but it still felt like a miracle. Last night the real snow had lasted for only a couple minutes, a freak temperature inversion that had shifted back into rain before long, but Alexa didn't think she would ever forget the magic of that moment, tipping her face back in the arms of the man she loved and feeling the snowflakes falling on her face.

Unfortunately, Callie hadn't seen the snow, fast asleep in her bed dreaming of Santa's arrival, so Elia had surprised them that morning with a little field trip. He'd pulled some strings with some of Elite Protection's high profile clients to get them access to the indoor winter wonderland. Callie was laughing shrilly as she cavorted in the fake snow with the children of TV star Ty Walker, who had arranged the indoor snow day.

The snow may be fake, but everything else in her life was incredibly real.

Elia, standing at her back with his arms snug around her. Real.

Callie, laughing and smiling like a girl who knew how much she was loved. Real.

And the way she felt about them both filled up her chest, making her feel like a helium balloon about to lift off. Very real.

She may or may not be able to patch things up with her father some day, but Elia had reminded her that she already had a family. She had Callie. She had Victor—who was more father to her than her own father had ever been. And she had him. What more could she ask for?

"You angling to move into my sweet digs at the North Pole?" Elia asked as Callie dusted some "snow" off her legs and wandered over.

Callie rolled her eyes, scowling. "You still aren't Santa."

"I don't know," Alexa argued. "He's pretty magical. Are you sure?"

The day certainly felt like it had been filled with miracles.

The locals in Tahoe had rallied around them. Apparently after the first photo had leaked, one of the vendors at the fair had called in to argue with a commentator on one of the twenty-four hour news channels and his defense of Alexa's parenting had become the reigning soundbite. Several gossip sites were already issuing retractions.

Her tour would happen after all, ticket sales stayed strong—but she and Victor had already been discussing how they could reschedule dates so she wouldn't have to be away from Callie as much, and figuring out ways for her daughter to travel with her when it wouldn't interfere with school.

She was worried less about staying on top as a pop princess and more about making sure she didn't miss another minute with Callie, but that didn't mean she would stop recording and performing. She already had plans for an acoustic Christmas album for next year. Inspired by a certain Santa.

Miracles everywhere.

A loosely packed snowball hit Callie and she dove back into the piles of snow to find the culprit, and Alexa couldn't fight a smile.

Elia leaned down so his lips were next to her ear. "I feel like I should warn you now, we're naming our first daughter Noel. And any boys will be Chris or Rudolph."

She laughed. "Aren't you getting ahead of yourself?"

"Do you love me?"

"I think I just might," she teased.

"Then what more do we need to know?" He swept her off her feet and into his arms. She laughed as he carried her beneath the snow machine that flung a dusting of fake snow over them. "Kiss me, Mrs. Claus," he demanded.

How could she possibly resist?

"Oh, *Santa*," she sighed dramatically, twining her arms around his neck and kissing lips that were smiling against hers, certain with Elia she had a lifetime of smiling kisses to look forward to.

Miracles everywhere.

THE END

ABOUT THE AUTHOR

Award-winning contemporary romance author Lizzie Shane lives in Alaska where she uses the long winter months to cook up happily-ever-afters. A three-time finalist for Romance Writers of America's prestigious RITA Award, she also writes paranormal romance under the pen name Vivi Andrews. Find more about Lizzie or sign up to receive her newsletter for updates on upcoming releases at www.lizzieshane.com.

ALSO BY LIZZIE SHANE

MARRYING MISTER PERFECT
ROMANCING MISS RIGHT
FALLING FOR MISTER WRONG
PLANNING ON PRINCE CHARMING
COURTING TROUBLE
ALWAYS A BRIDESMAID
LITTLE WHITE LIES
DIRTY LITTLE SECRETS
ALL HE WANTS FOR CHRISTMAS
THE DECOY BRIDE